MOTIVE FOR MURDER

Inspector Mallison was reluctant to arrest the murdered man's son, although the incriminating evidence was overwhelming: he'd been alone with his father immediately prior to the murder and there'd been a bitter quarrel; Goldstein was killed trying to alter his will — unfavourably for his son; the weapon, a desk paperweight bore the son's fingerprints, and his father had withdrawn financial support for a new West End play in which his son was to star. Yet still Mallison wasn't convinced . . .

JOHN RUSSELL FEARN
Edited by
PHILIP HARBOTTLE

◆

MOTIVE
FOR
MURDER

Complete and Unabridged

LINFORD
Leicester

First published in Great Britain

First Linford Edition
published 2012

Copyright © 1940, 1946, 1954 by
John Russell Fearn
Copyright © 2011 by Philip Harbottle

British Library CIP Data

Fearn, John Russell, *1908 – 1960.*
Motive for murder.- -
(Linford mystery library)
1. Detective and mystery stories.
2. Large type books.
I. Title II. Series
823.9'12–dc23

ISBN 978–1–4448–0996–1

Published by
F. A. Thorpe (Publishing)
Anstey, Leicestershire
Set by Words & Graphics Ltd.
Anstey, Leicestershire
Printed and bound in Great Britain by
T. J. International Ltd., Padstow, Cornwall

This book is printed on acid-free paper

Part 1

Motive For Murder

1

'Obviously telephoning when the blow was struck,' Inspector Mallison mused, as he swiftly reconstructed the crime. 'Fallen half across the desk, then slid sideways on to the floor, taking the pile of papers and the telephone with him. His weight smashed the chair as he went over; must be quite fourteen stone,' he judged, his eyes on the huddled body sprawled grotesquely in the shadow of the large desk.

He glanced up at the man beside him. 'I take it death would be practically instantaneous, Doctor?'

Doctor Frazer nodded.

'Certainly,' he concurred in thin, precise tones. 'The skull is badly fractured. He must have been struck with great force — a grim business, Inspector.'

The eyes of both men went to the heavy brass paperweight lying a few yards away.

'Grim enough,' Mallison agreed laconically, 'although in this case I don't doubt a good many people will sleep easier in their beds now that Goldstein's gone — moneylender, wasn't he?'

'I believe so.' There was distaste in the other's tone. The Inspector glanced at him a trifle quizzically.

'I never had much to do with him,' Frazer added hastily.

His manner was a trifle pompous. He was a man approaching sixty, of a stooping tallness, with a lean, rather harassed face, and a tight, humourless mouth. He looked the very antithesis of the Inspector, who was short and whose stoutness gave the impression of jovial good nature that the cold keenness of his grey eyes belied.

'Of course, we've been neighbours for years, as you doubtless know,' Frazer continued, 'but his occupation — you understand?'

'A usurer, of necessity, has few friends,' the Inspector agreed drily. 'Well, Doctor, I don't think I need trouble you further — you'll be a busy man, I know.'

4

There was a brisk dismissal in his tone. Frazer bowed gravely, then moved towards the door. The constable stood aside to let him pass.

Whistling softly beneath his teeth, Inspector Mallison took up his stand with his back to the open french window and surveyed the room.

His hat was pushed far back off his rather high forehead, and his clever eyes darted from side to side, noting the position of the desk with the doors and windows respectively.

The massive marble fireplace was on the right, the door leading into the hall in the left-hand corner of the wall opposite, which meant that it was at the back of anyone sitting at the wide desk, he noted. For the desk stood left centre and was set at an angle to the fire.

The room was thickly carpeted and furnished with solid, rather tasteless, comfort. There were dark velvet hangings at the windows.

In the wall on his left hand was a smaller door, leading apparently to an inner room. The Inspector crossed to it,

5

and glanced inside.

It was quite a small room and, judging by the fact that there was only the one door, the two had at one time been one larger room, from which the smaller portion had been partitioned off. The room contained a small desk with typewriter, a filing cabinet, and a small electric stove. There was a french window almost facing the door, which gave on to a narrow strip of garden, being set in the side of the wall of the house. Through it a boundary wall was visible, and beyond that a squat building of dull red brick. Probably Doctor Frazer's house, he thought absently, unless he lived on the other side.

He returned to the larger room.

'Well — I'd better hear what these women have to tell, Where are they?'

'In the room across the hall, sir.'

'Good. When Walker comes to do the prints and photographs,' he directed, 'warn him to be particularly careful of that paperweight.'

'Yes, sir.'

The constable sprang to open the door.

Mallison strode briskly across the hall, tossing his hat down on the hall table in passing, then tapped lightly on the door of the room opposite, and went in.

A strained silence greeted his arrival.

A middle-aged woman, obviously the housekeeper, sat huddled beside the fire. On the extreme edge of a chair in the corner, a man in earth-stained clothes sat awkwardly apart, twisting his cap between his hands. A tall, dark girl of about thirty-six stood staring out of the window, her fingers fiddling restlessly with the edge of the curtain.

Dusk was falling outside and the window framed that intense blueness which is the effect of a half-light outside when the room itself is in shadow.

The Inspector switched on the light and instantly the window became grey and colourless, and the room took on the aspect of a lighted stage.

Mallison's glance passed over the group thoughtfully. The older woman was stout to the verge of obesity, and showed a scared, grief-stained face, Both women were unmistakably Jewish, and the younger one had the striking dark hair and smooth, white skin of her race, and would have been handsome, but that she was so thin as almost to be emaciated. She met his glance with a firm coolness, and the Inspector caught the impression of an extreme capability.

The last of the group, Ernest Fletcher, the odd-job man, continued to stare stolidly at the carpet, his large, loosely jointed hands hanging awkwardly over his knees.

Mallison addressed the girl first.

'You, I take it, are the dead man's niece?'

She nodded.

He took out a pencil and notebook.

'Your name?'

'Rebecca Coel.'

'You live in the house?'

'Yes.'

'How many are resident altogether?'

'Just my uncle and myself,' she took his inquisition calmly. 'Zillah, here, is housekeeper, and we keep one maid, who's been out since lunch and hasn't come back yet. Those are all who live in.

Fletcher here comes two days a week and works in the garden, or does odd jobs about the house.'

'I see.'

He had jotted down all her replies in a swift, microscopic shorthand.

'Now, Miss Coel,' his keen eyes searched her face, 'I appreciate that your uncle's death will have been a very great shock to you, and I don't want to worry you unduly.' A grimness crept into his manner. 'But this is a case of murder, you realise that?'

From Zillah crouched by the fire came a sudden whimpering sob. He saw Rebecca Coel's hand tighten on the curtain, but her dark eyes intent on the Inspector's face were tearless.

'Yes, I realise it,' she said steadily.

'Good,' he exclaimed, relieved at her calmness. 'Then you'll understand how essential it is that you should tell me all you know.'

'I'll help you all I can.'

She came over and sat on the settee facing him. He saw that her eyes were feverish, and rather heavily shadowed.

She had a nervous jerky habit of touching her upper lip with her fingertips.

'Overwrought despite her apparent coolness,' the Inspector decided, and his voice was a little less peremptory as he continued:

'You were in the house when the murder took place, Miss Coel?'

She nodded.

'I was in the next room,' she said in a low voice.

'The next room?' There was no doubt that Mallison was startled.

'I was my uncle's secretary,' she explained simply. 'I was working at my desk as usual.'

He stared at her thoughtfully.

'Then you must have been aware of what had taken place, surely?'

'No. That's the amazing part about it — I heard nothing. The insistent ringing of the telephone was the first intimation that anything was wrong. I was typing, and at first didn't notice it. Then I realised that it was ringing, and thought uncle must have gone out of the room, so I went in to answer it. Then I saw him — '

She broke off, her face dead white. Mallison nodded sympathetically.

'No one was in the room?'

She shook her head.

'What did you do?'

The girl crumpled her handkerchief nervously between her fingers.

'I screamed and ran into the hall. Zillah came and I told her what had happened. We both went back into the room. Fletcher was there. He had heard my scream and had come in from the garden. I left them and ran next door for Doctor Frazer. He came straight away, said that uncle was dead, and that we'd better send for the police.'

There was a pause. Mallison looked at her searchingly.

'You heard no sound of a struggle — a fall or anything?'

'No — nothing at all. Of course, I was typing.'

He rubbed his chin.

'Amazing,' he muttered, then he bent forward in his chair. 'You say your uncle was alone in the room when you found him. There was no sign of his assailant.

Had anyone been with him as far as you know prior to the attack?'

The girl's hesitation was palpable. There was a short silence.

'Well, Miss Coel?'

'There was someone with him a short while before,' she said, reluctantly. 'But I'm sure he had nothing to do with the attack.'

'Miss Rebecca's right, sir. Mr. Jacob didn't do it.' It was the old housekeeper who spoke, and her agitation was painful.

'He didn't do it, I tell you. He couldn't have done — not Mr. Jacob.'

Rebecca Coel's calm was shattered by the old woman's outburst.

'No one suggests that he did,' she broke in violently. 'For heaven's sake pull yourself together, Zillah.'

Then she checked herself and strove for calmness. Again came that nervous flick of her fingers against her upper lip.

Mallison's earlier judgment of her was confirmed.

'Hm. I was right,' he thought. 'A mass of nerves.' Aloud, he asked mildly, 'Who is Jacob?'

Rebecca Coel's eyes avoided his.

'My cousin,' she said, reluctantly. 'Uncle's only son.'

A sharpness came into the Inspector's face.

'Goldstein's son, eh? That's interesting, and he was with him that same afternoon. How long had he been there?'

'Since three o'clock. He rang up just before lunch to ask whether uncle would see him.'

'What time did he leave?'

'I don't know.' Her manner was guarded. 'You see, I was typing — I didn't hear him go.'

Mallison stared at her thoughtfully. Then he turned to Zillah.

'You any idea when he went?' he asked brusquely.

The old housekeeper shook her head.

'Then he must have let himself out, eh?' he suggested, and she gave a frightened nod.

There was a short silence.

Mallison glanced shrewdly from one to the other, a possibility had presented itself irresistibly to his mind.

'What sort of terms were they on?' he asked, and the housekeeper's agitation told him without doubt that his surmise was correct. 'So, it's like that, eh?'

He looked evenly at Rebecca Coel.

'Hadn't you better tell me all you know?' he suggested. 'I appreciate that you're reluctant to say anything which might implicate your cousin, but evasion is useless in a case like this, and creates a bad impression. You can best help him by telling the truth.'

'I suppose it's bound to come out in time,' she agreed wearily. 'Just recently they'd quarrelled rather bitterly.'

'What about?'

'His engagement,' she said, reluctantly. 'Millicent Marsden, David's fiancée, is not of our faith, and uncle was violently opposed to their marriage. He was very orthodox in his views.'

'David?' the Inspector interposed swiftly. 'I thought you said his name was Jacob.'

'It is. David is his stage name — David Kant.'

'David Kant!' Mallison's lips pursed into a whistle, as he recognised the name of a young actor who had recently leapt to prominence, 'And he is Goldstein's son?'

She nodded.

'He refused to come into uncle's business when he left college,' she explained swiftly. 'He was crazy to go on the stage. He'd talent, too, and uncle recognised it and let him have his way, though he was bitterly disappointed. He told him repeatedly that he was a fool, but he gave him an allowance to help him over the difficult period. I think secretly he was rather proud of his recent success, but the engagement was a terrible grief to him. He wouldn't countenance the marriage at all unless the girl adopted our faith, which she refused to do, and David backed her up to it. That was what made uncle so terribly angry.'

'Was that the reason for their interview today?'

'Yes,' she admitted, uneasily. 'Uncle threatened to stop his allowance if he went on with the marriage.'

'Hm.' Mallison stared at her thoughtfully. The reason of her earlier reluctance to speak of her cousin's visit and the reason for old Zillah's agitation were now plain. He questioned her keenly about the interview, but either she knew nothing of what had transpired, or she was determined to give nothing more away.

'Come, Miss Coel,' he said, rather brusquely. 'You were only in the next room, and you'd be naturally interested. Do you honestly tell me that you have no idea how the interview went? Whether they quarrelled more bitterly or reached agreement?'

'I heard nothing,' she persisted.

The Inspector jumped to his feet and strode restlessly about the room. 'Pity we don't know what time he left. That might settle everything.'

Fletcher, who had sat all the time in silence, cleared his throat. 'I saw him leave, mister.'

Mallison stopped short and stared at him.

'Oh, you did, did you? Well, why the devil didn't you say so before?'

'You didn't ask me,' the man's voice was nettled.

'I was coming to you later,' the

Inspector said testily. 'What do you know about this business?'

'I know nothing,' the man replied stolidly. 'Except that I heard sounds of a quarrel and saw Mr. David leave.'

'Heard sounds of quarrelling, eh? From the study?'

Fletcher nodded.

'Hear anything of what was said?'

'No, sir — I was too far away for that, right at the end of the garden here, but I remember thinking that they must be having a rare set-to.'

'Yet, Miss Coel, who was only in the next room, denied hearing anything unusual,' he observed drily. 'Then what happened?'

'Soon after Mr. David came striding down the path. He looked rare put out, didn't seem to see me at all.'

Satisfaction showed on Mallison's face.

'Now we're getting somewhere. What time was this?'

The man scratched his head. 'I couldn't rightly say. Maybe about four o'clock. It wasn't long after when I heard Miss Coel screaming.'

'How long after?' The Inspector's question came like a pistol shot.

'Maybe five minutes, maybe longer. Not more than ten.'

'What did you do then?'

'Ran in through the window into the study. Saw the old man lying on the floor. Then Miss Coel came in with Zillah from the hall, as she told you.'

'Hm.' Mallison turned to the girl.

'Miss Coel,' he said grimly, 'I strongly suspect you of knowing more of this than you've acknowledged, but I respect the motives that have prompted your evasions. So I'll say no more at present, but I'll question you again later.'

'I can tell you nothing more,' she said, obstinately.

There came a knock at the door, and a man about thirty, of a lean, intent briskness, put his head inside

'What is it, Walker?'

'Note from the Yard, sir.'

Mallison tore it open, and read the message his face inscrutable, only a faint whistling between his teeth betrayed the importance of its contents.

'Miss Coel, I want your cousin's address.' His tone was peremptory

She gave it mechanically, and whilst the Inspector jotted it down Zillah watched his face with dazed, hopeless eyes.

He put the book away and regarded the two women.

'A message has just come through the Yard. Goldstein was 'phoning his lawyers when he was struck down. He was discussing an immediate alteration of his will.'

* * *

Mallison leaned back in his chair and looked at his superior.

'Well, sir, I think that covers everything.'

On the table between them stood a heavy brass paperweight. A number of photographs were scattered about, and there was a neat pile of documents, and a small, loose-leaved reference book bound in black leather.

'That's the result of over three weeks' intensive work. I've gone over the whole ground exhaustively, and I flatter myself that there isn't a loophole that hasn't been explored. There's nothing further left to do.'

'Except to issue a warrant for his arrest, eh?'

Mallison nodded sombrely.

'Yes,' he agreed slowly. 'That's all.'

There was no elation in his tone — rather a brooding disquiet.

Superintendent Barker, a man of sixty-five, with a square, dominant face and heavy lidded, intelligent eyes, leaned back in his chair and studied the Inspector shrewdly.

'Mallison, I don't understand your reluctance. From your marshalling of the case, evidence against young Goldstein seems overwhelming. He was alone with his father immediately prior to the murder. We have evidence of them quarrelling bitterly. The old man was struck down when actually telephoning his lawyers over an alteration to his will to his son's disadvantage. His fingerprints were found on the paperweight, which was obviously the weapon used. We also have to bear in mind the further fact that Goldstein was financing this new play in the West End in which his son was to take a prominent part, and that because of the dispute he had withdrawn his support, although the piece was already in rehearsal. He seems to have been determined to bring the boy to heel. Confound it! You have opportunity and overwhelming motive; cumulatively, it's simply damning.'

Mallison's jaw thrust out pugnaciously. 'That's just it ... It's so damned circumstantial,' he muttered.

'Most evidence in a murder case is,' Barker observed, drily. 'People don't usually arrange for an audience when they're about to kill someone. Hang it. There isn't a weakness anywhere.'

'There's one.' A new alertness showed in the Inspector's face. 'Take this paperweight, for instance.'

He tapped the lump of brass with his fingertips.

'Kant's fingerprints are on it all right. I don't deny that. They showed here and there.' He indicated the places with a pencil point. 'Now, if I was in a fury and had the impulse to use that as a weapon, I should pick it up like this.'

He scooped it up in the palm of his hand, his fingers clasping it firmly.

'You see where my fingers grip?' he pointed out. 'Underneath. Kant's prints were on the upper surface, which is perfectly consistent with his story that he merely fingered the weight as it stood on the desk whilst he was talking to his father.'

'I see your point, but Kant's hand is considerably smaller than yours,' Barker objected.

'I tried him with it,' Mallison put in shortly. 'He gripped it easily, and I contend that it is the more likely way.'

He stared challengingly at his superior. Barker, his face thoughtful, experimented with the heavy weight, grasping it first as Mallison illustrated, then picking it up from the top.

'You see it isn't impossible to grip the weight by the top, Inspector. The surface is sufficiently uneven to form a firm hold.'

'No,' was the reluctant response, 'but I

think it's damned unlikely.'

'Maybe. But it's a small point. It certainly isn't sufficient to justify any further delay on our part, Mallison.'

Barker's voice was authoritative. The Inspector stroked his chin.

'I don't like it,' he muttered uneasily. 'Everything fits together too slickly. I distrust circumstantial evidence; always have and always will.'

'The old complaint, Inspector, eh?' Barker interjected quizzically. It was often a point of contention between them.

Mallison shrugged his shoulders.

'I wouldn't hang a sick dog on circumstantial evidence. Still, I admit it looks black enough in this case — poor devil.'

He slumped gloomily in his chair.

Barker trifled idly with a small, silver pencil.

'This young fellow seems to have impressed you pretty favourably, Inspector.'

Mallison shot him a glance from under his heavy brows.

'He didn't strike me as a murdering

type,' he admitted guardedly. 'But anybody's liable to strike someone in a sudden fit of passion, and there was provocation enough. No, I'm too old a hand to be swayed by appearances. It isn't that.'

He heaved himself out of his chair.

'Well, I suppose there's nothing more to be said. The law must take its course.'

Moodily he commenced to gather the papers and photographs together. Last of all he picked up the loose-leaved reference book, and flipped the pages over idly.

Neatly tabulated, it contained an alphabetical list of all the moneylender's clients.

'I thought we might have discovered something from this little lot. Some poor devil who'd been driven to that last desperate way out. Plenty of motive here, I should say, for murder. But despite the most searching inquiries, we couldn't trace a thing — '

He had been turning the pages rapidly through his fingers as he spoke. Suddenly he paused, held by a sudden intentness.

He flipped the pages over again, then he turned back to one near the front and scrutinized it carefully, finally holding it up to the light. Then he turned the next page and held that up to the light, too, and yet another.

'What is it?' Barker asked curiously.

For answer, Mallison put the book in the other's hand.

'Examine that page closely. Notice anything?'

After a close scrutiny, Barker shook his head.

'Hold it up to the light — and the next page. Now do you see?'

Comprehension dawned on the other's face. 'The watermark is different.'

'It is,' came the keen reply. 'That page is foreign to the book. It's newer than the rest, but it's been so well fingered that it isn't perceptible. I must have had it in my hand a dozen times and never noticed it. It's the edge that's given it away. It's whiter than the rest. When I was flipping the pages over just now it showed as a faint white streak.'

Mallison gazed at it fixedly, a single

page with half a dozen names and addresses, and a letter of the alphabet printed in red in the top right-hand corner.

Barker, leaning across the desk, watched him keenly.

'You think the page might have been substituted deliberately?'

'I don't know,' the Inspector's voice was absent. 'The explanation for it may be a perfectly simple one, and have no bearing on the case whatever. On the other hand — obviously it opens up a new line of inquiry.' He glanced at his superior slyly, and his voice, when he continued, was bland. 'I suggest that the question of Kant's arrest should be held up until I've had time to pursue it.'

There was a nettled expression on the Superintendent's face. He believed that Mallison's unwillingness to force a conviction on overwhelming circumstantial evidence alone was making him grasp at trifles.

'Who was in charge of the books?' he asked shortly.

'The dead man's niece, Rebecca Coel.

We've been through her testimony, sir. She was in the next room when the murder was committed, you remember.'

Mallison reached for one of the portfolios, swiftly turned the pages and laid it on the desk before his superior.

'Yes, I remember.' Barker tapped his teeth with the pencil as he studied the memorandum. 'You were sceptical of her evidence, believed she was trying to shield her cousin, eh?'

'She was so anxious not to admit anything incriminating against him — overanxious. It had the effect of damning him completely. She seemed a cool customer, but overwrought, a bundle of nerves — hm, I wonder?'

'When did she give you the book?'

'The next morning when I went through the files with her. She's extremely capable. Everything was in scrupulous order. If the substitution was deliberate, she'd have ample time to do it.'

He straightened up and looked at the other questioningly.

'Have I your permission to look into this, sir?'

'I suppose so, damn you!' Barker replied testily. 'Though it's a hundred to one it's a mare's nest. I'll give you a couple of days.'

'Right — it's a bargain.' There was satisfaction in Mallison's face. 'It hung together altogether too neatly. I'd a hunch that there was a snag somewhere if only I could get my finger on it.'

★   ★   ★

His hat pushed characteristically to the back of his head, Mallison coldly surveyed the group of people assembled by his order in Goldstein's study. It was afternoon of the second day following the interview in Barker's office.

Rebecca Coel was sunk deep in a heavy armchair over by the fireplace. The Inspector's eyes rested on her thoughtfully. The pallor of her face was startling and intensified by the dark rings beneath her eyes. Her hands, clasped tightly in her lap, twitched with overstrung nerves.

David Kant stood leaning against the mantle and staring sombrely at the carpet. His fiancée, Millicent Marsden, sat on a low stool at his feet. She was a graceful, fair-haired girl with a soft mouth and steady eyes, which were fixed now with a look of dumb, anxious appeal on Mallison's grim face.

Zillah occupied the other easy chair and a scared-looking maid sat uneasily on a straight-backed chair at her elbow.

Ernest Fletcher completed the group, standing stolidly beside the wide desk. Deprived of his cap, his ungainly hands hung at his side, and with one bony finger he explored ceaselessly the seam of his corduroy trousers.

There was a complete silence, and the ticking of the clock on the mantelpiece was plainly audible. Mallison glanced at it irritably. The hands stood at ten minutes to four. He pulled his own watch out of his pocket and compared them, then stared out into the garden.

Kant glanced up.

'May I ask what we are waiting for, Inspector?'

'We're waiting for Frazer.' Mallison's voice was testy. 'I want everyone here who was — ' He broke off as his quick ears caught the click of the front gate. 'Ah, here he is.'

'In here, Doctor,' he called through the open window. Frazer entered from the garden. He had been hurrying and was out of breath.

'I'm a little late, I'm afraid,' he apologized punctiliously.

'That's all right, Doctor,' the Inspector said, with an attempt at geniality that did nothing to conceal his irritation. 'I'm obliged to you for coming. I know you're a busy man, but as you were near at hand, and there's a small point on which I shall need your testimony, I thought I might venture to trouble you.'

'No trouble at all,' was the grave response. 'I'm glad to give any assistance I can.'

The doctor took a seat at the far side of the desk, and surveyed the others curiously from under his shaggy brows.

Mallison took up his stand with his back to the window and cleared his throat.

'Nearly a month ago, in this room, in broad daylight, a man was brutally murdered. He was struck down, as you know, by the heavy paperweight standing on the desk there, and killed instantaneously, or presumably instantaneously. I'd like your opinion on that later, Frazer.'

The doctor nodded without speaking, and the Inspector continued his harangue.

'Obviously our first suspicions were directed against his son here, who was alone with his father immediately prior to the attack, and was known to have been quarrelling with him violently. Who, moreover, had the strongest reasons for desiring the old man's death.' His voice was calmly impersonal.

'Kant's testimony,' he continued, 'is that his father was still alive when he flung out of the study in a fury, and Fletcher here saw him striding down the path. Now the time factor in this case is very important. Kant states that he left his father just as he was about to carry out his threat of ringing up his lawyer and making an immediate alteration to his will!'

Mallison's glance swept round the circle of faces.

'Goldstein made that call we know. We have testimony from his lawyers, Soames and Grant, that the call was put through. He was actually dictating the terms of a new will disinheriting his son when he was struck down — '

The disclosure caused a startled stir, and everyone glanced involuntarily at the young man's set face, then dropped their eyes uneasily.

'So that Soames, all unknowing, actually heard the murder committed,' Mallison pointed out imperturbably.

Frazer leaned forward in his chair.

'Is that an actual fact, Inspector?'

Mallison nodded.

'Extraordinary!' the doctor muttered under his breath.

'Yes. It's the most amazing thing I've ever encountered in all my twenty years at the Yard,' the Inspector admitted. 'Not that he was able to help us, unfortunately.' His voice was rueful.

'All he could tell us was that Goldstein's voice broke off abruptly. He heard the sound of a fall and groans. He thought the man had fainted, and unable to get any further reply, he notified the exchange. It was the exchange that was responsible for the insistent ringing of the second line 'phone which attracted Miss Coel's attention.'

He cast a swift glance at the girl in the chair, whose eyes were intent on his face.

'Which, incidentally, bears out her statement, for the girl at the exchange heard Miss Coel scream, realised something was amiss, and notified the police.'

Mallison noticed Rebecca's hands, which had been gripping the arms of her chair, suddenly relax, but his face was inscrutable as he continued:

'However, although Soames was unable to give us any clue to the identity of the murderer, his evidence was of vital importance. I referred just now to the time factor. His evidence established without a doubt that from the time the blow was struck to the moment that Miss Coel's screams announced the discovery of the murder, at least ten minutes elapsed. The delay, of course, was due to his getting in touch with the exchange. Now, bearing in mind Fletcher's statement that from Kant passing him on the path roughly ten minutes elapsed before Miss Coel's screams in the study attracted his attention, one thing seems certain.'

He paused, there was a deathly stillness.

'Either,' Mallison continued inflexibly, 'Kant killed his father, or he must have been struck down almost immediately following upon his departure from the room.'

'Which I take it is just another way of saying you believe me guilty,' Kant flung at him. His finely cut, handsome face was haggard.

'I didn't say so.'

'No.' The young man's voice shook, but he fought to control it. 'But you're hinting that it's mighty improbable that anyone else was hanging around just choosing that particular second to kill him. Well, if you're here to arrest me, cut the talk and get on with it,' he said, desperately. 'I suppose you have your warrant with you.'

'David, please.' Millicent's voice was scarcely more than a whisper, but it checked his outburst.

'I'm sorry,' he muttered, and passed his hand nervously over his face. 'I guess I forgot myself, but these last few days have been hell. Everyone here believes that I killed my father, and I don't seem to have a dog's chance of proving my innocence.'

'Not everyone, David,' Millicent corrected. Their eyes met and his face lightened.

'Bless you,' he whispered unsteadily. Impulsively she reached up and slipped her hand in his, then turned confidently to the Inspector, but Mallison didn't notice. He was watching Rebecca Coel.

The girl had sunk back deep into her chair and put her handkerchief to her shaking lips. Her cousin's outburst appeared to have completely unnerved her.

'Would you like a drink?' he asked, curtly.

She opened her eyes and stiffened under his scrutiny.

'No. I'm all right now.'

She pulled herself together with a marked effort.

Frazer leaned forward, frowning.

'Miss Coel has only just recovered from a severe illness, Inspector. She really isn't fit — '

But the girl herself interrupted him.

'Thanks, I'm quite recovered now.' She spoke with some of her old assurance but again came that jerky flick of her fingers, against her mouth. 'I'm quite ready to hear what else the Inspector has to tell us.'

Mallison picked up a slim leather-bound book from off the desk. For all her show of confidence, Millicent watched him with wide, anxious eyes.

'It's a peculiarity of one British form of Justice,' the Inspector continued, 'that we always give a suspect the benefit of the doubt, however black circumstances may appear against him.

'Mr. Kant himself has pointed out,' he observed drily, 'that it seems very improbable that anyone should have been hanging about here ready to seize upon that peculiarly opportune moment for killing Goldstein. But we were forced to consider the possibility, however remote it seemed. One of the first things I did was to go through the books dealing with the dead man's accounts with Miss Coel here, who is, I may say, a most efficient secretary. This is a reference book which she placed in my hands, containing an alphabetical list of all Isaac Goldstein's clients.'

He turned the pages reflectively. 'Obviously, Goldstein's death was to the advantage of all these people, some of whom were in debt to him to a very considerable amount. Naturally, it is here that our first suspicions would be directed. We made the most exhaustive inquiries into all these people's movements, but,' he shut the book with a snap, and laid it down on the desk, 'there wasn't an atom of proof against any one of them.'

There was a short silence, then Kant spoke harshly.

'So where does that leave us?'

Mallison didn't answer. He moved away from the desk and stood regarding Rebecca Coel steadily.

'Miss Coel, you were working in the next room when this murder was committed, and for a time we seriously considered the possibility that you yourself had killed Goldstein, knowing full well that suspicion would inevitably be thrown on to your cousin.'

She started violently, and her hands clutched convulsively at the arms of her chair.

'But on consideration,' Mallison continued, 'we realized the absurdity of such a suspicion. You had no motive for desiring your uncle's death. On the contrary, the very strongest reasons for preventing it at that particular moment, for on Kant's disinheritance, you yourself became Goldstein's heir, which makes your attempt to shield your cousin all the more creditable,' he added.

'You still persist, by the way, that you heard nothing of the quarrel between them?'

'I heard nothing,' she interrupted tonelessly, 'as I told you before.'

'Our experiments do not bear out your statements,' he said, drily. She watched him mutely as with the utmost deliberation he produced a folded paper from his pocket.

'Miss Coel, you did your best to save your cousin,' he said gravely, 'but you failed. I have a warrant for his arrest.'

He put his hand on Kant's shoulder, and Millicent eave a stricken, heartbroken cry, but Rebecca was on her feet, screaming in sudden frenzy.

'No — no!' she screamed wildly, and a look of triumph flashed into Mallison's face.

'Who killed Goldstein?' he snapped. She put her hand to her throat. She was staring over the Inspector's shoulder. A dawning hopelessness showed in her eyes.

'I can't tell you,' she whispered, and before anyone could catch her she slid, a crumpled heap, on to the floor. Mallison dropped on to his knees.

'Quick, Frazer,' he shouted, and the doctor hurried to his assistance.

Between them they lifted the unconscious girl back into her chair. Then Mallison spoke to the others impatiently.

'Brandy — quick!' he shouted, but Frazer shook his head.

'She couldn't take it, I'm afraid,' he said, gravely.

'But you've got to get her round, man,' the Inspector urged. 'She's got to tell us who killed Goldstein.'

The doctor straightened up, and his face was dubious.

'I doubt whether she'll be fit for any further questioning tonight.'

'A faint, eh?' Mallison's voice was truculent. 'You're sure it's genuine?'

'It's complete collapse, due to over-strain and excitement,' Frazer stated. 'Hardly surprising under the circumstances. We'd better take her to her room.'

'A moment, doctor.'

Mallison bent and lifted one of the unconscious girl's eyelids, then glanced up questioningly, A curious grey pallor became evident in Frazer's face.

'That's no faint, doctor. Look at the pupils. It's coma brought on by excitement following an overdose of cocaine. She took it behind her handkerchief when Kant here was working himself up into hysteria.'

As he spoke the Inspector's blunt fingers had been busy probing in the upholstery of the deep chair. He drew out a small gold box with a screw lid, and held it out mutely in his palm.

'Any medical man would have suspected it, but you were slow to diagnose her condition, Frazer, although you yourself supplied her with the drug — oh, no, you don't!'

This last came through his teeth as he countered the almost maniacal suddenness of the other's attack.

A chair went over as they struggled. The women screamed as Kant leapt to the stout Inspector's assistance. Helmeted fingers appeared like magic from the hall and garden. Handcuffs were snapped round Frazer's wrists, and still struggling, he was hauled to his feet.

Mallison straightened up, breathing heavily. Then for the second time he produced the long official document out of his pocket.

'I have a warrant here for your arrest, Frazer. You murdered Goldstein, and this wretched girl was your accomplice.'

He looked into the distorted face before him, and his eyes were bleak and merciless.

'There's only one motive strong enough to make a person insensible to the claim of overwhelming financial advantage, affection or human pity; it is the frenzy of a hopeless drug addict threatened with cessation of their supply. That was the hold you had over this wretched woman here. She was torn between her natural affection for her cousin, and the fiendish craving which I suspect you've deliberately fostered in her for your own ends.'

He turned to the others.

'This murder was entirely premeditated,' he explained. 'This man was deeply in Goldstein's debt and getting desperate. He learned from the girl of the interview arranged between her cousin and his father. It was the opportunity he had been looking for. He used the tradesmen's entrance and entered Rebecca's room through the french window. There's a privet hedge outside that acts as a convenient screen so that he stood little chance of being detected. He was in the girl's room all through the interview, and heard everything that took place. When Kant left, he quietly opened the door, crept up behind Goldstein as he telephoned and struck him down. He was wearing gloves so that he left no prints. Then he left the house in the same manner as he had entered it. Probably he arranged with Rebecca not to give the alarm until he'd had time to gain his own house. A matter of a few minutes only, but the ringing from the exchange timed things for him nicely.'

He regarded the accused man steadily.

'You planned a clever crime, Frazer, and you almost succeeded in fastening it on an innocent man, but you overreached yourself. You were too thorough. I'm always suspicious of evidence that hangs together too slickly. I can't leave it alone until I find the flaw — '

He nodded at the slim, black reference book lying on the desk.

'That was the flaw. I don't know when you arranged for the substitution of that other page, so that your name wouldn't appear in the records. Possibly the girl was typing it whilst you were listening to the quarrel that was taking place in the other room,' he hazarded, and a look of sudden fury in the other's eyes told him that his guess was right. 'She fingered the page well. Frazer, but the edge was clean — a little thing, doctor, but it's going to hang you — '

'You can't prove — '

'Quite right, doctor,' Mallison's interruption was genial. 'All this is mere conjecture. I admit that. But now the girl's ready to talk, and that makes all the difference. Her testimony is all I want.'

He made a sign to the men about him. 'Better take him away.'

★ ★ ★

'A sheer stroke of luck, really, sir,' Mallison protested modestly, later in Barker's room, after receiving his superior's congratulations.

'If I hadn't ransacked the girl's desk in an effort to find the file from which that extra leaf had been taken, I might never have got on to it. She must have spilt the stuff at some time. Just a few white grains. I understood then that nervous habit of hers of flicking her fingers against her nostrils. The unconsciously acquired habit of a drug addict.'

A frown drew his thick brows together. 'I'll recognise it again when I see it — after that it was easy. The question of supply put me on to the doctor, together with the fact that the substituted reference sheet was for the letter F. I made inquiries and found he'd attended the girl through a severe illness, and drugs had been used to deaden her pain. That was the start of her craving, I suppose, as it has been with many another poor devil, but there's no doubt the scoundrel deliberately fostered it — I don't know yet how deeply he was in Goldstein's debt, but I've discovered his particular vice — gambling. He can't leave the cards alone.

'Not such a mare's nest after all,' he observed, and glanced slyly into his superior's face. Barker regarded him oddly, then gave a wry, good-humoured grin.

'You win,' he said briefly, and a smile of intense satisfaction spread over the Inspector's broad face.

Part 2

White Outcast

1

The Attack

The summer evening had fallen with quiet calm over Manhattan Island when the flyer suddenly appeared. On the less densely populated outskirts of New York City, families on their apartment roofs, either reclining or taking supper, saw the flyer first as a tiny oval against the crimson flush in the west.

Nobody paid much heed. Flyers of various designs were common enough over the rearing super-city of this advanced age. Only one thing seemed queer. The flyer was not heading toward any of the 2,000-foot high directional towers that would guide it to the landing bases; and yet it was not lost. Its steady movement showed no sign of hesitancy.

Here and there men and women glanced at one another in surprise. Then throughout the entire block of apartments — known as Square 14 — there was sudden consternation as the flyer came to a halt a thousand feet above.

Hundreds of pairs of eyes stared upward at a flat, aluminum-coloured belly. A light of blinding amber winked momentarily within it — and then hell broke loose! Square 14 — the entire vast cube-like apartment block — split asunder with a tremendous din.

Bricks, steel girders, black glass façades, whole roofs even, mingled with the shattered bodies of human beings in a blast that shook the heavens. Avalanches of debris thundered back into the streets a thousand feet below. The calm peace of the summer evening vanished with diabolical suddenness.

Here and there trapped survivors in the wreckage caught a glimpse of the mystery flyer as it swept downward. But now, suspended from its base, were twin horseshoe magnets — magnets that dove into the wreckage with ceaseless purpose, magnets of tremendous heaviness that hurled many a running figure into eternal darkness.

There was something incredible about the way those magnets plumbed the wreckage as demoralized human beings tried to find out what it was all about. For ten minutes the flyer darted about, driven with amazing accuracy, avoiding the stunted ruins that might have smashed it in pieces.

Then the magnets withdrew suddenly and the flyer whirled through the dusty haze, finally screamed to the ground on the top of plaster and gray boulders.

Arthur Corton, an uptown bank clerk, pinned under the wreckage by some miracle of fate had his head free. He was possibly the only man who saw what happened. Through the dust he glimpsed an open airlock in the ship. From it a figure slowly emerged. He was almost naked, save for a loincloth; human in outline, but of a doughy white colour. His skin hung in pasty folds. His face was flattish, almost bestial, with spreading nostrils and eyes as colourless as glass.

Corton struggled frantically to free his

pinned legs. Failing, he lay there gasping as the mysterious individual scraped hurriedly amidst the ruins with a tiny magnet in each hand. The man came and went with desperate purpose; then all at once stopped and listened.

All of a sudden he raced back to his ship at top speed, jumped in and slammed the door. There was a titanic gust of hot air. The flyer lashed forward with staggering speed into the murk and deepening darkness.

Moments later a party of rescuers came plowing through the ruins.

'Here!' Corton shouted desperately. 'Here! I'm being crushed to death!'

The rescue squad asked no questions, got immediately to work. As it proceeded, Corton heard through his blur of pain the screech of alarm sirens, the blasting roar of stratosphere police planes, the distant crackle of static from electric guns slamming death charges into the upper heights.

Manhattan was prepared now — but the preparation was too late. The unknown craft had vanished utterly, and some seven hundred innocent persons were dead or brutally mangled. Then for Arthur Corton too the world was suddenly dark and quiet.

Between spells of coma Arthur Corton was afterwards aware of faces grouped round his bed — grim, determined faces, and one in particular which reminded him of a granite statue. He recognized the blunt, stern features of Vincent Burke, head of the Scientific Investigation Bureau's homicide squad.

Burke was speaking in his clipped, purposeful voice.

'You've been saying things, Mr. Corton — delirium, maybe; but if you can make it, I'd like to know more. Something about a ship and a man with doughy features — '

'That's — that's right.' Corton breathed hard. There was damnable pain eating through his chest. In remote horror he realized he might never be sound again.

'I — I saw *him* — for a moment. About six feet tall, nearly naked, colour of wet bread — '

In jerking gasps Corton went on to tell

of the magnets, of the searching.

'I don't know who — ' he started to say, and then he relaxed and became motionless.

Burke compressed his lips and turned away, rubbing his heavy jaw slowly as his associates and the newsmen gathered round him.

'Exit the last survivor,' he observed laconically, shrugging. 'Come on, Sphinx, we've things to figure out at headquarters. No statement yet, boys,' he added briefly.

'Sphinx' Grantham, his personal assistant, with features about as communicative as those of his stony superior, followed his chief out of the hospital. As usual, he made no observations. It was his job to answer, not to comment.

As the fast official car whirled the two police officials back through the traffic, the radiophone in the roof came into life.

'Calling Chief Inspector Burke.'

Burke switched on. 'Burke answering. Go ahead.'

'Operator 9 reports further activity by unknown invader north of the city. In ruins of Square 14 again. Ambulance and rescue squads were overcome by gas and smoke barrage, but Operator 9 caught a brief glimpse of visitor. Six feet, white all over. Operator 9 took his aura frequencies on the detector. Invader got away. That is all.'

Burke switched off with a gloomy smile. He glanced across at Sphinx' overlong, expressionless features.

'About the queerest set-up I've struck yet,' Burke said briefly. 'Sounds like an interplanetary visitor of some sort — but why the hell does he have to cause all this trouble? Why destroy Square 14 and all those poor devils?'

'I guess we're paid to find that out,' Sphinx replied logically.

'Yeah — and we will!'

Burke broke off as the car drew up with a screech outside headquarters. He stalked through the building to his private office and snapped on the night duty button. In five minutes twenty men had assembled — trained, picked men, always at the service of the Bureau in the night hours.

'Now get this, boys.' Burke stood facing them, his face grim. 'We're up against either an alien murderer or else an insane man. If the former, he's the first visitor from another world, but that doesn't make him less dangerous; the opposite, in fact. We've got to find him!

'In this city we've brought crime to a low level, and no saboteur is going to start upsetting order while we're around! Seven hundred people dead — *seven hundred!* And all for no apparent reason! So hop to it, men! Contact stratosphere headquarters, contact Operator 9 and get the frequencies of this Unknown from him. Check everybody you think would have even the slightest bit of information.

'There's a chance that our killer is some crook in fantastic make-up using an extra fast stratoship mistaken as a space-machine. It's a possibility — so work on it! Get him — dead or alive!'

Without a word the men filed out. Burke turned and flipped a coin on the desk.

'Get me a packet of cigarettes, Sphinx. I've run out of 'em. Can't think without 'em — '

Sphinx took up the coin, then paused and tossed it back.

'You can't get away with that one,' he observed gravely. 'Better give me real money.'

'Huh?' Burke looked up impatiently, studied the coin in surprise. It was not money at all; it looked rather like a badly scratched token of some sort.

'Somebody gypped me,' he observed, thrusting the coin back in his pocket and tossing over another.

Sphinx went out just as 'Big Boss' Calman came in. Calman was the head of the entire Bureau, controller of every department, the brains behind the brains. But he knew the individual values of each of his chief inspectors, allowed them free rein unless circumstances demanded his presence.

'Everything set to go to work on this invader?' he asked Burke briefly, surveying him with his pale grey eyes.

'Yes, sir — everything,' Burke nodded. 'The boys just left, and I've plans of my own to work out.'

'Okay — if you need me at all, don't

hesitate to call. I'm going home. See you tomorrow.'

'Good night, sir. If it's possible to get that killer — well, we won't be asleep at the switch, Mr. Calman.'

2

The Work of a Fiend

For quite a while Burke sat pondering. Mechanically he took the cigarettes Sphinx Grantham brought in for him. He was still musing by the time Sphinx had come up from the night canteen with sandwiches and coffee. Then the radio bell rang with strident force.

Startled, Burke turned and switched on the receiver.

'Hello there, Burke. Listen carefully. This is Calman. I'm speaking from a public radio box. Come down to Intersection 30 right away. I have found something pretty queer. I believe it's the guy we're looking for — What? That's what I said. He's lying dead among the girders supporting the 30th Pedestrian Gallery. Step on it!'

'Right away!' Burke closed the switch. 'Let's go!' he added briefly, and Sphinx was right beside him as they raced down the corridor.

The fast police touring car whirled them through the floodlit and now almost deserted streets, drew to a squeaking halt under the mighty girders of the 30th Pedestrian Gallery. Calman was there, waiting by his car, the headlights of which were turned upward.

Calman said briefly, 'Take a look!' and nodded his head.

Burke narrowed his eyes. A white figure, practically naked, was suspended motionless in the crotch formed by two immense X girders, caught round the waist. His legs and arms dangled grotesquely.

'Looks like our man,' Calman said grimly. 'I've been up to take a look. Come and see for yourself.'

He led the way up the emergency stairway. Presently Burke stood looking down on that nameless thing so obviously dead. A gaping wound was on the forehead, from which blood still oozed in a dribbling stream. The entire figure, save for a loincloth of curious leathery substance, was naked. It was human enough in form, except for the ridged thickness of the skin. It was a skin utterly unlike that of a human being, rough and coarse as though afflicted with some mild form of elephantiasis.

'Queer how he got here,' Burke mused.

Calman said, 'As I figure it out, he must have been creeping along the Pedestrian Gallery above, slipped, and — Wham! Anyway, it's the man. His ship ought to be somewhere around. I saw him hanging there in the lights from my car while I was heading home. Better have the boys look around for his ship, and we'll cart him to the morgue and see what sort of a being he really is. Come on.'

Struggling and shoving, it took the three of them their united strength to lift that gross, heavy body. They managed it finally and staggered down the stairway with it, dumped it in the back of the roomy police car.

'I'll come with you,' Calman said, withdrawing from his own car. 'I've told the boys to take my car home. Let's be moving.'

He slid in beside Burke and the engine roared.

Burke swung the steering wheel. Sphinx Grantham sat motionless in the back of the car, his deadpan face unmoved by the close proximity of the weird corpse. He gazed straight ahead at the swirl of lights as Burke stepped on the gas down the official traffic-way — 90 . . . 100 . . . 125 . . .

There were no limits on this wide, light-drenched expanse; a vast bridge, one of many crossing the newly created river dividing Manhattan in half where once Madison Square had been. Now Long Island Sound and the Hudson were united to facilitate watercraft.

Below, the river shone like molten lead. The girders of the bridge zipped past in trellises of mist. Then suddenly the front of the car was no longer there!

A terrific explosion hurled the hood skyward; flame and impact split the engine asunder. In two mad seconds Burke was aware of the slender rail at the base of the girders as it hurtled to meet the shattered car.

The machine plunged through. Flung clear, Burke went flying through space. Somehow he straightened his legs as he fell, went headfirst into the water and plunged below.

Dazed but unhurt, he bobbed to the surface.

'Sphinx! Calman!' he bellowed, fighting desperately against the current.

'Here!' Sphinx yelled, about fifty yards away. 'All right?'

'Find Calman!' Burke shouted.

He threshed around, calling his chief by name. Sphinx swam level after awhile, blood and water trickling together down his face.

'Guess he's gone,' he panted. 'Lend me a hand, Burke. I got cut on the head.'

Burke caught his assistant as he sank weakly. Though even their united efforts were feeble, they managed at last to struggle to the mud of the bank, crawled up and sat there trying to get their breath back.

'He must have gone down with the car and the corpse,' Sphinx panted at last, holding his damaged forehead. 'I don't suppose the corpse would float out anyway; it was jammed pretty tight in the back. But Calman could have gotten free; it was an open car.'

'Unless the initial explosion killed him,' Burke said soberly. He gazed up at the break in the rail where the car had plunged through.

'That,' he said slowly, 'was no accident. Cars don't blow up in these days; they're fireproof. Either something was planted in the engine while we looked at that corpse on the gallery, or else — By God, Sphinx, I'll find out who's behind all this if it kills me!

'Calman's dead, and we'll have to get the dredges to work mighty quick if we want to save that corpse, too. Come on. We've got to report this. After that we'll attend to your head.'

Burke turned to stumble up the bank, then about-faced sharply at the sound of threshing water behind him. Something was struggling in the river. It came closer, visible as a man's head in the light of the bridge.

'Calman!' Burke cried. He plunged out

waist-deep into the river again, helped Sphinx to drag in their almost exhausted chief.

'Thanks, boys.' Calman staggered up beside him. 'Hell, I thought I was finished! I went under with the car and my belt got caught. Anyway, I made it — '

Without further comment the three of them floundered up the bank, headed for the nearby radio box and contacted headquarters.

'Well?' Burke asked grimly, as they stood waiting under the official lamp. 'Any theories?'

'None that I'd like to express right now,' Calman answered tersely. 'Either this — this white outcast is dead, or he isn't. Depends on whether that explosion was timed for after his death, or whether the figure on the gallery girders was put there as a decoy.'

'You mean there might be *two* outcasts?' Sphinx demanded blankly.

'There might be. Damned if I know the answer. Well, we'll see what happens next. If there are no more attacks on us, then we know it was a posthumous effort to kill us, and it failed. If otherwise, we'll begin a manhunt that the town will never forget!'

Calman stopped speaking as two spots of light enlarged into headlamps along the bridge. That was the police car they'd ordered.

The following day, as the broadcast media and morning newspapers headlined the explosion at the bridge and later commentators began referring to the 'White Outcast' — as the unknown marauder had now become known — three grim men at Bureau headquarters went over every detail of the problem to date.

They found no definite clue, however, for there seemed to be no motive in the senseless destruction of Square 14. The effort to destroy the three leading lights of the Bureau was more understandable — but again it proved nothing.

Was the White Outcast still alive — or dead? There constituted the main problem, and until the killer perpetrated some further act of mischief, the matter was unsolvable. Certainly there was no trace of his spaceship anywhere.

Burke gave the necessary instructions for the river to be dragged, and toward four in the afternoon the salvage was complete. The derelict car was removed to the official headquarters and the corpse jammed inside was dumped on the slab in the morgue. Dr. Rayfrew, the chief medical examiner, went to work at once.

'In the meantime,' Burke said, 'I'm going to take a look at that car. Maybe we can find out something.'

'If you do, notify me immediately,' Calman told him. 'I'm going uptown to take a look into the Matthews case. You know where to reach me if necessary.'

Burke nodded. He and Sphinx adjourned to the yard behind the building to survey the soaked, muddy ruin of the car that had nearly been their coffin.

'If you expect to find anything in that, you're a better man than I am,' Sphinx commented.

'You never can tell — ' Burke muttered.

He went to work methodically, tore out the sodden upholstery, stared at the utterly shattered engine. Presently he pointed to the remains of the carburettor. It was of the usual advanced type common to modern engineering.

'Notice?' he asked briefly.

Sphinx gazed at it earnestly, but he shook his head.

'So what? It's black around the broken edges. The fuel mixture must have caught fire.'

'Yes, but *how*? A modern carburettor can't catch fire! An outside agency had to do it. Somebody arranged a spark of some kind that fired the fuel. The enormously powerful mixture we use went off like a bomb and — blooey!'

Burke went back to his labours. Finally he took out what remained of the metal front floorboard. Half of it, on the left where he had sat, was smashed into jagged remains. But the other half was clear except for a neat hole, perhaps three inches in diameter; a hole apparently bored by heat, for the edges were obviously blackened.

'Either I'm crazy, or — ' He broke off at length, handed the sheet of metal to

Sphinx. 'Put this in cold storage somewhere. I may think of something later to
match that hole.'

'Crazy,' Sphinx observed solemnly, 'was
right.'

By the time Burke had finished probing
around, Sphinx had returned. With him
came the lean-faced medical examiner,
Dr. Rayfrew.

'Say, Burke, you'd better step into my
autopsy room. Plenty that is queer about
that stiff you brought in.'

Once inside the place Rayfrew nodded
to the dead thing on the slab, then
handed over a collection of X-ray plates.

'You'll see for yourself that the organs
of this creature are utterly different from
ours. Liver, heart and stomach are there,
to be true — but not in places we ever
heard of. Then the bone structure is
different, too. Shoulders pretty weak, legs
strong. I can't place it at all. As to the
cause of death, it was probably cerebral
hemorrhage caused by a terrific blow on
the head. Perhaps the girder of the
Pedestrian Gallery. It had to be a tough
blow. This creature's skin is so dense, you

couldn't hurt him by ordinary methods. Queer, also, are the main nerve branches.

'I believe he might be able to control the nerve endings of his skin, like a chameleon does. The skin has a highly sensitive under-surface. Probably got that way controlling the pigment. Perhaps, if his home planet were distant from its sun, a natural power on the part of an inhabitant would be necessary to make his skin supply these deficiencies.

'Well, anyway — thanks,' Burke said, still puzzling. 'He's a mystery. Was he the only one, or were there others? Where's his ship got to? The boys who think the pyramids are a puzzle should try this one! Well, let's go, Sphinx. I've things to do. Get rid of the body in the lethal chamber, Doc — no sense in embalming it for future use: may contain dangerous germs. And hang on to those X-ray plates.'

Renfrew frowned. 'The scientific community won't like that. As the first alien, they'll want to examine — '

'You've already done that,' Burke snapped. 'They can study your findings.

Get rid of that body before it starts a plague!'

'Very well,' Dr. Rayfrew nodded.

In his office again, Burke switched on the intercom.

'Terry? Hop down to the river again with the boys. Cover all the area where you dug up the car, send down relays of divers if you have to. Anyway, keep on dredging until you discover something that looks like a ray gun.

'You what? No, I don't know what a ray gun looks like. It's like a torch, I suppose. Use your imagination. It's only a hunch of mine, but keep on looking until you're cross-eyed, if you have to. Yes, I know it's soft ooze! Use hand and mechanical dredgers. Sift the whole bed of the river if you have to — Right!'

'This is absurd!' Sphinx protested. 'Why a ray gun? We don't even use 'em yet.'

'No, but I have an idea the aliens do. I figure it was a ray gun or something very much like it that fired our carburettor. It wasn't an ordinary gun, because the hole in the floorboard is too wide to show the passage of a bullet. A savage blast of flame could have made that hole.'

'You mean a ray gun was fixed there, somehow?'

'Just what I mean. And since it wasn't found in the car, it must have got dislodged when the car fell in the river. Unless it was blown to bits in the explosion. But somehow,' Burke finished slowly, 'I don't think it was.'

Sphinx Grantham scratched his head. 'You got me,' he said. 'I — '

He paused as Burke lifted the telephone. He rang a number, the private waveband number of all wristwatch telephones owned by agents of the Bureau.

'Hello there, 9? Burke speaking. Any dope yet?'

'Not yet, sir. We checked up on all likely crooks for their aura frequencies, but there was nothing doing.'

Burke frowned. 'So we'll try another angle. The Outcast is a mystery if he still lives. We're not dealing with a known factor at all. Start contacting the rest of the men in the Bureau and make your plans for finding his ship. I believe it ought to be around somewhere. Report to me if you find anything.'

'Right, sir!'

Burke switched off, then on again as the emergency light went up. It was Police Officer Higson. His voice sounded excited over the speaker.

'Better come right away, Mr. Burke. I'm over on Sector 5. Something queer here. An antique dealer has been attacked by the Outcast. Come right away, or it'll be too late. I think he's passing out — '

'Okay.' Get a statement from him. Be right with you.'

Burke slapped on the office phone. 'Tell Mr. Calman to meet us right away at Sector 5. No time to explain. Urgent!'

He glanced at his assistant. 'Come on, Sphinx!'

They hurried into the waiting car. It swung around and bolted along the official traffic-ways at top speed. Neither of them gave a thought to a possible repetition of the previous night's outrage. It was the job of the Bureau to ignore personal danger — and they did, successfully. Nothing untoward happened.

They drew up on the other side of the city ten minutes later, to find a cordon of police keeping back curious sightseers from one of the oldest stores in this part of town, a section given over almost entirely to antiques of the 20th century and preceding years.

Inside the shop, Officer Higson was kneeling on the floor with his notebook beside an obviously dying man. The victim spoke weakly, looked up as Burke came in. He was oldish, possibly sixty, with crinkly brown beard around a lean face.

'He saw the Outcast, Inspector — ' Higson started to say, but Burke waved him aside.

'What happened?' Burke caught the man by the shoulders.

'I — I was over there, at the desk. Things were quiet. I — I was busy — with my hobby — '

'Hobby? What hobby?'

'He writes messages on grains of rice and things,' Higson volunteered.

'Miniature calligraphy, eh? You mean you were doing that when the Outcast came in?' Burke looked rather incredulous.

'Yes, sir. I — I hardly heard him come. Must have been watching me for — for he suddenly put out his huge hand and — and snatched up the grain I was working on. Then he fired something at me — a sort of dart — '

The man relapsed into momentary silence. 'He stole my rice, my instruments, and — and ransacked the place,' he finished dully.

As Burke puzzled, frowning, there came the approaching scream of an ambulance siren.

'You're sure it was the Outcast?' Burke snapped.

'I'm certain. Big, dirty white — only wearing a loincloth — '

The man sagged weakly, licking his lips. Burke stood up, scratching his head and watching as the man was lifted into the waiting ambulance. Then he swung around to the doctor in charge.

'Get Dr. Rayfrew from headquarters to

attend to this man personally — nobody else. Tell him I said so.'

'Very well, Inspector.'

Calman came in hurriedly then, gazed around at the disordered shop. 'What's going on here, Burke? Came as quick as I could. The Outcast again?' he asked seriously.

'Yeah — and he's no more dead than I am!' Burke fumed. 'But the absurdity of the thing!' he went on helplessly. 'The crass lunacy of the creature! He came in here and stole some rice on which that poor devil had been writing; also frisked the apparatus. That fellow does microscopic engravings for rings and things — you know, calligraphy. His hobby seems to be printing hundreds of words on grains of rice.'

Calman nodded slowly. 'I know the kind of thing you mean. But how did the Outcast get in here without being seen? Busy street outside.'

'There are alleys at the back,' Sphinx spoke up. 'I saw them as we came up. The Outcast could have skulked around there and come up from the river somewhere.

Anyway, we know he's alive — even if we can't fathom his motives.'

'This,' Burke said grimly, 'is going to take more thinking than I'd figured. Maybe we'll get a lead when we know what it was the Outcast fired into that guy. I think it may have been a dart or something. Well, let's get back.'

3

Episode at the Bridge

The antique dealer died on the way to the hospital. Just the same, Dr. Rayfrew followed out orders and made an autopsy. He returned to Bureau headquarters with a grim face, entered the private office where Burke, Calman and Sphinx Grantham were debating the problem.

'Well, Doc?' Burke looked up anxiously.

'Poison,' Rayfrew said. 'But no poison I ever heard of, and certainly not of *this* world! Introduced by a small splinter. Latent in effect, which was why the victim took a while to die. Guess that's all there is to it, gentlemen. I'll analyze the poison if you want.'

Burke pursed his lips. 'I don't think it signifies — All right, Doc, go ahead.'

Burke looked grimly at Calman and Sphinx as the medico went out.

'Does it occur to you that we perhaps

have a clue?' he asked slowly, after a moment or two. 'This White Outcast is searching for something — that much we know. But doesn't his theft of microscopic writing on a grain of rice show that it is something small he's looking for? And don't forget he ransacked the store looking for God knows what. He used magnets when he blew up Square 14. That seems to suggest it's something metallic he wants.'

'There's something else,' Calman said. 'The Outcast obviously got the dealer's name from the directory. He's listed as about the only expert in miniature calligraphy in the city. Only that seems to show that the Outcast knows English.'

'Yeah,' Burke mused and leaned back to think. After a bit: 'He smashed down Square 14 and searched through it. Now just what was peculiar about Square 14? Same as the rest of the city, wasn't it?'

'There's one thing, but it's probably unimportant,' Sphinx said. 'It was the last Square to be built. Don't you recall the row there was over the brick delivery for the foundations? Clay pits went haywire or something and they had to import bricks from the Worth Clay Concession in the New Jersey section.'

'Yes, I remember that.' Burke pondered for a moment, then he said, 'Sphinx, I've got an idea. It may be wrong, but anything's worth a try. I want you to get in touch with the contractors who built Square 14 and find out everything about it; where every scrap of material came from. Maybe we can get some idea then of what the Outcast is driving at. It should at least extend our field of activity, anyway. We're stymied as it is.'

'Right!' Sphinx nodded, and went out without another word.

'Something else occurs to me, too,' Burke continued, as Calman sat with puckered brows. 'This Outcast possibly knows that Operator 9 recorded his frequencies on the detector. Next thing we know, the Outcast will try to steal that detector, or destroy it somehow. He might, to save himself from ever being found out.'

Calman glanced up. 'I didn't know you had the Outcast's frequencies. It ought to be a cinch now to — '

'It isn't, sir. The Outcast watches that. Even if he disguises himself, he takes good care to keep out of sight and out of reach of that detector. It would be safer locked away in our vault, where he can't ever get it.'

'Well, you might do that,' Calman agreed.

Burke made to rise, then glanced up as the door opened and Terry Walton of the Salvage Department came in. Without a word he laid a mud-stained, water-choked tube with glittering metal ends on the desk.

'Exhibit 'A',' he observed laconically. 'This what you were wanting, Burke? We dug it out of the river just as you ordered.'

Calman caught it up and stared at it. 'What the blue hell is this?'

'Ray gun,' Burke said briefly. 'I'll look at it later. Keep it safe till I get back, Terry. Thanks a lot.'

'You certainly work in a strange way, Burke,' Calman commented, as they went down to the inspector's car. 'Incidentally, where are we going now?'

'To pick up that detector from Operator 9. At the moment, he'll be at his usual station.'

Burke started up the engine. In a moment or two they were cruising at a leisurely 100 m.p.h. along the official traffic-ways.

'Just how did you know about there being a ray gun in the river?' Calman mused. 'That's pretty smart detective work, I'd say.'

'Pure assumption, sir. I usually play my hunches. I couldn't visualize anything else blowing up our car engine. There was a hole in the right-hand side of the floorboard, too. Being metal, only a ray gun — or something like it — could have burned through it.'

'In that case, it must have been fastened somewhere near where I was sitting. Hmm — funny I never noticed it.'

Burke shrugged. 'Plenty of room to conceal it, and it was dark, too. Obviously it was put there while we dragged the corpse down from the gallery girders.'

He said no more, and Calman sat rubbing his chin mystifiedly. The car went on, stopped at last in the middle of the great bridge where there reposed a base box: apparatus not unlike a railway signal box of old. There were seventy of these in the city, all told, from which the various operators of the Bureau controlled their particular quarter of the metropolis. They were in truth the police precinct stations of this advanced year.

'Shan't be a minute, Mr. Calman,' Burke said, leaping out. He raced up the steps into the small building and found Operator 9 inside, busy as usual at the control switchboard.

'Evening, Inspector.' He got to his feet.

'Better hand over that frequency detector, 9,' Burke said. 'There is a chance that Outcast knows about it and will try and get it. He may blow you sky high, even. I don't want to lose that record, whatever else may happen. I'll take it back to headquarters.'

Operator 9 turned to the heavy safe and brought the delicate instrument to view in its mahogany case.

'Frequency reading is registered on the tabulator, sir. Safety catch is down at the moment. Release that and she'll jump right away when you come within six feet of the man you want.'

'Yeah, yeah. I know all about it, son.'

Burke picked up the case and headed for the door. Just as he passed through the opening, he fancied he heard a scream. He frowned, raced down the steps. At the bottom of them he stopped dead, as he came in full view of the bridge road.

The car was still there, Burke noticed quickly, but so was something else. A mighty figure of dead white, wearing only a loincloth, was standing intently at the bridge, watching something in the river below.

Burke's eyes narrowed as he took in the details of that bulky, doughy body. Without a sound he edged toward the car, keeping his eyes on the hideous creature. Instinctively he lowered the detector into it — when all of a sudden the Outcast swung around. Burke gave a little gasp. The creature was almost nauseating in appearance, like something fashioned out of white, clammy clay. The pale eyes stared with hypnotic fury.

'Get away from here, Mr. Calman!' Burke yelled. 'Let me handle this fiend. We can't afford to lose you, too!'

Then, praying that Calman would follow his plea and duck out of the car, Burke centred all his attention on the loathsome white body. The pale cold eyes held him for a moment as though in a trance.

'Operator 9! Quick!' Burke yelled, breaking the spell. Then he swung about with a gun levelled in his hand. But he had not the time to fire it. With an incredible leap, probably because he was accustomed to a far heavier gravity on his home planet, the Outcast leaped clean over the top of the low-built car and landed in front of Burke.

Simultaneously a fist struck the police inspector violently in the face. Burke went hurtling backward against the ironwork of the bridge. His gun went sailing into space.

Operator 9 appeared suddenly, brandishing two formidable-looking guns. Burke doubled up his fist and drove it with all his power into the leering face in front of him. The doughy features jolted under the onslaught; then Burke saw the big hands tugging at a little pouch on top of the loincloth. A splinter, coated with venomous red, came into view.

Sight of it spurred Burke to desperate activity. He squirmed free from the bridge rail, rained blows on that mass of white, dense flesh, even gained the ascendancy for a moment.

Operator 9's gun fired noisily — once, twice, three times. One bullet hit the ironwork; the other two presumably drilled into the Outcast, but seemed to make no impression beyond inciting the fiend to greater fury. He charged on Burke like a whirlwind.

Burke spun around, slammed up his fist, rocked the Outcast like a pendulum. But more than that Burke did not attempt. That splinter was no thing to trifle with! He jumped to the bridge parapet, shouting back to Operator 9.

'Drive like hell — to headquarters! Take the detector!'

Then Burke leaped, just missing the

Outcast's clawing hands. He made a neat clean dive and plunged into the river far below, rose up shaking the water out of his eyes. As he emerged he heard Operator 9 starting the car engine from above, could see the Outcast looking down at him from the bridge.

Slowly Burke swam to the bank, climbed up it. When he looked back at the bridge again, the Outcast had gone. The chief inspector smiled bitterly to himself and made his way to the nearest official intersection on the lower walks.

Burke landed back at headquarters looking bedraggled and feeling ill. He found Operator 9 already there, waiting, the undamaged detector in his possession.

'It meant letting the Outcast escape to follow out your order,' the youngster said briefly. 'I just made it!'

'Good man.' Burke scooped back his hair. 'You can get back to your post now, and notify every man to keep his eyes peeled. We know the Outcast is in the city, anyway. I'll take charge of this detector.'

He swept the instrument up and went out to the Bureau vault down the corridor. When he came back into the office, he gave a start of surprise. A drenched figure was standing there, clothes tattered and torn, eyes gleaming with anger. It was Calman, physically unhurt, but in a pitiable state of attire.

'In a little while,' he said slowly, 'I shall get thoroughly burned up if I drop in that damned river again. So he got you, too! I leaped for it before he had a chance to ram a dart in me. I just let out one mighty yell to try and warn you, then chose the least resistance. Got out at the south end.'

'Then I guess you didn't hear me yell,' Burke acknowledged grimly. 'When that devil loomed up before me, I didn't even glance inside the car to see if you were there. Well, anyway, sir, you escaped, and that's the main thing. By the way, Mr. Calman — that killer must have known somehow of what I've intended doing.'

'I've realized that,' Calman nodded, 'and it's something I can't understand.'

'I've got one or two ideas doped out,' Burke admitted, 'but they can wait for awhile. I'm going home for a change of clothes before I get busy again. Six o'clock now. Be back at seven. Maybe Sphinx Grantham will have got some information by then, too.'

He turned impatiently and swung out of the office.

4

The Decoy Theft

It was exactly 7.00 p.m. when Chief Inspector Burke returned. He found Calman absent, but the chief had left word that he had departed on an urgent mission with Dr. Rayfrew. Burke wondered vaguely what it could be.

Taking advantage of the brief lull, he picked up the ray gun from Terry Walton's department and spent half an hour making experiments on his own. He came thoughtfully back to the office to find Sphinx Grantham lounging around, munching a sandwich.

'Well, find out anything?' Burke asked shortly, tossing the ray gun on the desk.

'Yes — but nothing of much use, I'm afraid. Say, I hear you and Calman were attacked by the Outcast this afternoon and — '

'Forget it! What did you discover?'

90

Burke snapped impatiently.

'Well, I found out that, as I had figured, most of the bricks in the foundations of Square 14 were made of clay from the Worth Concession in the New Jersey area. It seems, though, that several men went to the Worth works and asked where the clay from a certain section of the concession had ended up.'

'And they were told it went into Square 14?' Burke asked quickly.

'Yes, that's right.'

Burke snapped his fingers. 'Now get this! Something was in the clay of the Worth pits which the Outcast wanted. He found it had been used — at least, that part which he wanted — in the bricks of Square 14 foundations. So he wrecked Square 14 to try and find whatever it is he seeks. Remember the magnets he used?'

'It's an idea, sure. But who were the other people who made the inquiries at the Worth works?' Sphinx asked shrewdly.

'I believe,' said Burke, 'that 'the other people' was probably the dead Outcast we found on the gallery. He could be made up to look like an Earthman, and he could adopt various different disguises.'

'He could at that!' Sphinx whistled. 'Then this other fellow who keeps attacking you and Calman and murdering obscure people — '

'He, I imagine, was the partner of the chap on the gallery, and for some reason did him in. I'm sure I'm right on that point. And so far, the Outcast hasn't found what *he* wants.' Burke broke off and smiled grimly. 'And we don't know what it is, either.'

'Something small, hidden in clay.' Sphinx mused perplexedly. 'Probably something with minute writing on it, if the attack on the calligrapher is any guide.'

Sphinx gave it up with a shrug and glanced at the ray gun.

'Find out anything about this?' he asked.

'It was the thing which set our engine on fire, sure as fate. The area of the beam — I've fixed it up again so it works — exactly matches up with the size of the hole in the floorboard. It went through the metal in a second, smashed the carburettor, with which it was in a direct line, and exploded the fuel mixture. It was so arranged that — '

Burke glanced up impatiently as the chief keeper of the safety vault came in.

'Mr. Burke — the detector's gone!' he exclaimed hoarsely.

'What!' Burke yelled. 'You damned, confounded idiot! Didn't I tell you to — '

'Yes, yes — to guard it! I know — and I did! You put it in the safe, and I've sat there every minute myself, looking in the safe at intervals to make sure — '

'*All* the time?' Burke demanded.

The guard gulped a bit. 'Except for an interval of about ten minutes when I was called to the checking room. Somebody was on the telephone and wanted the criminal record of Henry Walford. I was the only one that could give it. When I came back to guard the detector again, it had gone. That was just now. It's half an hour since I answered that telephone call.'

Burke thumped his fist slowly on the desk.

'Did this person at the other end of the wire thank you for the record when you'd finished?'

'I don't remember it, Mr. Burke. I just reeled it off — and you know what those records are. Takes ten minutes or so to do it — '

The man stopped, astounded. 'Good heavens, you don't mean I was drawn off to recite all that stuff and there was nobody listening on the other end!'

'Who,' Burke asked slowly, 'asked for the record?'

'Chief Inspector of Sector 20. Come to think of it, it struck me as rather queer at the time that he should want such a record. But — '

Burke whipped up the telephone, got the inspector on the wire. Sphinx and the vault keeper stood listening to Burke's clipped remarks. And the guard's face grew drawn with anxiety.

' — so you didn't, eh? Don't even know Henry Walford? Okay, that's all I wanted to know.'

Burke lowered the phone. 'Keeper,' he said grimly, 'the inspector did not ring you! He never even heard of Henry Walford. It was a great idea to take up your time and keep you out of your department — but nobody listened to your recital. And since there is a Henry Walford record in the files, you thought it was all on the up-and-up.

'But it was somebody else who asked the question! And only the oldest employees in this organization, like you and Sphinx and Calman, and I myself — together with some twenty-five other employees in other departments — know about the Henry Walford case. Some-where among these thirty old employees is the one who rang you up!'

'But nobody but the Outcast would want to steal that frequency detector!' Sphinx cried. 'You're not suggesting the Outcast is among our own staff, surely!'

'No, I'm not suggesting — I'm telling! How else could the Outcast know our plans so well! Who else but one of the staff could think up a trick like the Henry Walford record! Of course' — Burke gave a faint smile of triumph — 'I fully expected the detector would be taken. It confirms a theory I'm working on.'

He eyed the vault keeper steadily for a moment. 'You can get back to your job,'

Burke said quietly.

'Yes, Inspector. I can't begin to say how — '

'All right; all right. Forget it. Now, Sphinx — '

Burke broke off rather impatiently as Calman came into the room.

'Burke, you'd better come along to the morgue. We've just brought in a fellow attacked by the Outcast this evening. The police called Dr. Rayfrew and I went along with him, since you were away.'

Burke followed immediately with Sphinx at his heels. The man in Rayfrew's autopsy room was pretty elderly, plenty knocked about, but still alive.

'He's all right,' Rayfrew said briefly, 'except for bruises. About the first víctim to survive the Outcast, I guess — except you and Sphinx and Calman.'

'I went for the Outcast with an electric gun,' the latest victim panted. 'That scared him a good deal. And hurt him too, I think! It saved me from getting a dart of some sort. What? My name's Bradshaw. I'm a scientist, an inventor.'

'Are you listed in the directory of

occupations as a scientific inventor?' Burke asked keenly.

'Certainly I am. That was how the Outcast found me, I presume. I live in an isolated, old-fashioned place near the ruined Square 14. I was in my laboratory when the Outcast broke in through the window. He spoke to me — in English!'

Burke's eyes gleamed. 'Then what?'

'He said he had heard — probably through the television and newspapers — that I had invented a machine capable of producing long-range heat rays. That is quite true; but I invented the machine for peaceful purposes, mainly with a view to opening up the Arctic for exploitation of its mineral resources.

'I know plenty of warmongers on this world would like that ray of mine for destructive purposes. Well, sir, to my utter amazement, the Outcast said I had stolen the secret of my invention from his medallion, that it was one of his own twelve scientific secrets. He demanded I hand the medallion over.'

'Medallion!' Burke cried. 'So that's what he's looking for!'

'Naturally,' Bradshaw went on, 'I denied all knowledge of a medallion. Furious, he flew at me and I hit him. Then he pulled out a dart. I realized ordinary weapons were of no use, but an electric gun I had handy kept him away.

'Had I not been in my laboratory, I'd be dead now — Well, gentlemen, he fled. I summoned the nearest policeman to come and attend to me; I was pretty well knocked about, I can tell you. Then Dr. Rayfrew came finally, and Mr. Calman.'

'Your home, then, is about ten minutes away from here by fast car?' Burke asked thoughtfully.

'About — yes.'

Burke got slowly to his feet from the bedside chair.

'Mr. Bradshaw, it is evident that by a coincidence you happened to have made a machine identical with one supposed to be the secret of the Outcast — in formula form, at least. The secret of this machine, together with eleven other secrets, is impressed on a medallion. Hence, the theft from the calligrapher, in the hope that it might be there.'

'Say, that's right!' Calman cried. 'What else?'

'Sphinx found out enough to show me that this Outcast, either by accident or design, planted a medallion in the clay on the site that is now the Worth Concession. It's a comparatively recent site, remember. The clay the Outcast wanted had gone when he returned; it had gone into the bricks of Square 14. Result — the attack. Thereafter, a desperate search for the medallion and its twelve scientific secrets.'

'Then where *is* the medallion?' Calman demanded. 'Isn't that the next point? I think — '

'I believe I know where the medallion is,' Burke answered slowly. 'And I believe I can make the Outcast come and get it — this very evening!'

'You can!' Sphinx cried. 'But — but how?'

'You'll see.' Burke glanced around. 'Mr. Calman, I'm requesting you to order all members of the Bureau who have been in our employ over ten years, to be present in the assembly hall by 9.30. There will be around thirty, including ourselves.

'You're the chief, so the order had better come from you. I'll produce the medallion, all right, and I'll so arrange it that the Outcast will be bound to come for it.'

5

Metamorphosis

Those of the staff whom ten year's service designated were not at all keen on Burke's scheme, but since Calman gave the order, there was nothing for it but to turn up. Thirty or so employees — all of them who knew of the Henry Walford case — presented themselves in the big assembly hall by 9.30.

Calman was there, on the platform. Around him were one or two officials, Sphinx Grantham and Dr. Rayfrew. Burke arrived last by the rear door, looking very resolute and keeping his right hand in his pocket. He raised the other for silence.

'In this room,' he said slowly, 'are thirty-four people. I checked them as they came in. Every one is human — except one! I have publicized the fact in the last hour that the medallion is here tonight for the Outcast to come and get.

'So the Outcast is with us, and I warn him that I have the whole building surrounded by guards. But now I must make a confession. I have no medallion. In fact — I don't even know what it looks like!'

There was a tense silence. Calman broke the spell finally.

'I'm afraid I don't get this at all, Inspector.'

Burke's voice was harsh with purpose. 'The idea, Mr. Calman, is to make sure the Outcast is here. And he is. He knows we are right on his tail, and only by guaranteeing him the medallion would he be sure to come. Otherwise, he would probably have made a run for it before being caught and exposed.'

Burke paused and walked slowly across the stage. Then suddenly he whipped his right hand from his pocket. There in his palm was fisted the ray gun with which he had been experimenting. He levelled the weapon steadily.

'All right, Calman! Stand up!' Burke snapped.

'Me?' Calman cried. 'My good man, have you lost your mind?'

'Show's over, Calman. You're all through. *You are the Outcast!* And this ray gun of yours is the only thing your blasted flesh will wilt under! This — and an electric gun!'

Calman got up slowly, his eyes hot. 'Now look here, Burke, I can stand just so much nonsense! This is absurd!' he exclaimed. 'You're overwrought, Burke! Why, you must be seeing things!'

'Yeah?' Burke made a signal. From behind the stage curtains a technician emerged, carrying a frequency detector. Burke motioned him to hold it up.

The audience plainly saw the red register needle tally exactly with the blue frequency reading, previously recorded, as the instrument came near Calman. Indisputably Calman was the White Outcast!

'Aura frequency detectors never lie, Calman,' Burke snapped. 'You are the Outcast — and I've known it for some time! But I wanted to be absolutely certain. I found out quick enough when you stole a detector from the vault. Knowing the safe combination we use, it was simple enough, wasn't it? But you did not know I had put *another* detector in the vault with a phony number-frequency on it!

'The real detector was carefully put aside for an occasion like this. I had to manoeuvre things so I could get a reading without your being aware of it — and believe me, it took some doing. You made the Henry Walford phone call. You killed the *real* Calman on the night we found that awful-looking body in the Pedestrian Gallery girders. You killed Calman as he went home!'

'Calman' breathed hard. Suddenly there was a hoarse shout from the audience. Even Burke got a sick feeling in the pit of his stomach. For with a slow metamorphosis, Calman began to change into something revoltingly different. His features slackened and smeared, became doughy white. His flesh thickened oddly.

In four minutes 'Calman' had gone and the White Outcast — dressed in the lounge suit he'd stolen from the real

Calman — stood in his place. Even the weird creature's eyes had gone several degrees paler by inner control of iris pigment.

'All right, you win,' the Outcast said, without anger. 'I thought I was a good scientist — but you're one better than me. Why shouldn't I admit it?' He sat down heavily, shaking his head. 'I don't begin to understand how you knew.'

Burke's voice was hoarse from the strain he'd undergone. 'I didn't suspect you until Dr. Rayfrew said the Outcast might be able to control his nervous system after the fashion of a chameleon. He might, in other words, be able to metamorphose, to change himself, at will. Then Dr. Rayfrew told me of the possibility of extreme toughness.

'I figured out that an explosion — like the one in the car engine — would be unlikely to hurt you, Outcast, but very probably would kill Sphinx Grantham and me. It was worth your risk, anyway. The floorboard hole was just as I expected it would be had you had a ray gun or something similar in your hand. It would be hidden from my view by the darkness in the car.

'Well, I had the river dragged and a ray gun was turned up. If, as I suspected, you were the Outcast, you could not conceal the weapon in your pocket; because when you came out of the river, your clothes were clinging to you and the bulge would have shown.

'Since you were with us all the time we got the other Outcast from the gallery girders, you had not had time to fix anything in the car beforehand.'

'How do you know that body was a so-called Outcast, as you say?' the alien said softly. 'How can you be sure it wasn't Calman himself?'

Burke snorted. 'Don't be a fool too, Outcast. How could Calman have been metamorphosed into such a revolting mass of flesh — even by you? There are still some things that can't be done!'

'Indeed?' purred the Outcast. 'Well, I really must not spoil your fun. Continue, Inspector.'

Burke bowed mockingly. 'Thanks so much for your permission.'

His voice grew harsh again. 'Yes, I suspected you, all right. I knew that if you thought the frequency detector was in your grasp — which it was, in the vault — you would spare no pains to try and steal it, destroy it to make yourself safe. You did — but you took the wrong one!

'To make doubly sure of being rid of the two most likely to find you out — Sphinx and me — you continued your efforts against me when I went to get the detector. You got rid of your clothes somehow and metamorphosed yourself into your normal Outcast appearance. You looked realistically over the bridge at a mythical Calman who might have fallen into the water. You did the same thing when you attacked the antique dealer, I presume.

'By tonight I knew what you were looking for. Because of the medallion pretext, I made sure you'd be here. What I do not understand is, why you didn't kill off Sphinx Grantham and me with darts in the first place. It was your logical way out.'

The Outcast smiled bitterly. 'Too

obvious. It would have thrown suspicion on me. What I really wanted to do was to become undisputed head without you two being in the way. Some time ago,' he went on, 'I was fleeing through space from an enemy, returning to my home planet. It became essential that I get rid of the medallion of secrets as quickly as possible.

'I came to Earth, marked the spot where I had buried the medallion, and went on again without anybody on this planet being aware I'd landed. When matters calmed down, I was ordered to recover the medallion, never to return to my world until I had done so. It contains secrets of war engines that I stole from this enemy, who was pursuing me. I was allowed one companion.

'We arrived here and found changes in the clay site where I had buried the medallion. My companion and I spent some weeks learning your language by listening to radio and television broadcasts. Then my assistant, metamorphosed to look like an Earthman, started to make inquiries. We finally discovered the medallion was probably among the bricks of Square 14.'

The Outcast sighed as though in mild regret. 'My companion was against ruthless destruction, so I killed him. Then I destroyed Square 14 but failed to find what I wanted. Even though, were the medallion lying in the ruins, my magnets would have dragged it to view.'

The Outcast took two small horseshoe bars from his pocket and then replaced them.

'I had then to decide how best to find out where the medallion was. How better than as the head of the Scientific Bureau? They, in an effort to catch the White Outcast, might discover the medallion's whereabouts quicker than anybody.

'So, having studied Calman carefully beforehand in readiness for such an emergency, I took his place — killed him on the night you found my companion's body on the gallery. Calman's body I merely rayed out of being.' He said it coolly, unemotionally.

'One point,' Burke put in. 'Why did you change back into your Outcast pose when you made your attacks on the antique dealer and the inventor? Could you not have done such things as Calman, made your search under the pretext of police routine?'

'I could, yes. But while you were around, I knew it would arouse your suspicions if the chief of the Bureau started doing that kind of thing. Better to do nothing that the real chief wouldn't bother himself about.'

Burke nodded slowly. The Outcast went on calmly, in a matter of fact manner.

'I used my dead companion as a dupe, certainly. As I have already said, I tried to be rid of you and Sphinx Grantham without casting suspicions on my own bogus identity. Once I got the Bureau under my control without you two worrying me, I could probably track that medallion down in no time.

'I tried all likely people — or rather, I intended to. I only managed a calligrapher and an inventor before you caught up with me. I felt certain the inventor was the one because, according to newspaper reports, his invention was identical to the likeness on the medallion.'

'These twelve inventions,' Burke mused. 'I presume that every detail of each one is on the medallion in microscopic writing?'

'Exactly. The actual machinery can only be built with the medallion formulae. Otherwise, we only know what the inventions are — without knowing how to construct them.'

Burke said, 'Had you told us what you were seeking, to begin with, we would have helped you.'

'I think not.' The Outcast shook his head. 'Twelve engines of destruction would interest the war-loving scientists of this planet far too much. Such men could have become enemies of my own world at a none-too distant date. No, it was better I found the medallion intact, with its secrets unrevealed.'

He got slowly to his feet. Then suddenly he whipped back his sleeve and rammed something into his arm. Too late, Burke dashed forward to get a look at the tiny splinter.

'For an Outcast to die when his

mission has failed is surely logical?' the alien asked quietly. 'I have fought for my planet; you for yours. Both of us, I think, have lost.

'You wondered about my spaceship. It is in orbit nine hundred miles from Earth. It can only come down when this is operated — '

He whipped an object like a watch out of his pocket, fiddled with its tiny instrumentation, flung it on the boards and ground it under his heel.

'I have sent my ship on a course that will take it into the sun. You will have to solve interstellar space travel for yourselves,' he added dryly.

Suddenly he fell back into his chair, breathing hard. With a final convulsive movement he became motionless and relaxed.

Burke turned away quietly.

'Cigarettes, Sphinx. I want to think,' Burke said, as they went back to the office. He flipped a coin on the desk.

'Okay — but I wish you'd use real money.' Sphinx held up the dud coin for the second time in two days.

'Oh, hell — ' Burke began irritably. Then suddenly he snatched the coin from him and stared at it; at the roughed surfaces smothered in tiny, microscopic lines.

'My God!' he gasped.

Without another word Burke raced to the autopsy room in the morgue, where the Outcast's body lay. Rapidly he searched out the small magnets from the pockets. Instantly the coin clung to them.

'That's it!' Sphinx yelped. 'The medallion! Even when he was near you, your pocket held it in, stopped the thing from contact with the magnets. Lord, if you'd only known! If *he* had only known! But how did you ever come to — '

'How should I know?' Burke asked quietly. 'Dug up by workmen, I suppose. Handed around as a false coin, got into my loose change somewhere. I may have had it for ages. Funny as hell, isn't it?'

Burke smiled faintly as he gazed on the Outcast's dead face. 'You know, the fellow was right in some things,' he added.

'About war-mongering, for instance — Never mind those cigarettes right now, Sphinx. We're going to the river bridge. I've something I'd like to throw over the parapet . . . '

Part 3

He Walked On Air

1

Jarvis Downing, research scientist, quietly faced Doctor Adam Henderson, the world's greatest brain-specialist.

'I'm going to need your assistance soon, Henderson,' Downing remarked quietly, then began to slowly pace the great library. 'I've overtaxed myself through the years, and now something's happened to my brain. I saw a specialist today.'

'Yes?' The pale, unsentimental eyes of Henderson turned to follow his pacing friend.

'I have an incipient tumour on the right frontal lobe of my brain. Only one man dare remove it — you, of course.'

'I see,' the specialist said slowly, and studied his cigar.

Suddenly Downing ceased pacing. 'Henderson, do you think, if you operated, that I might live after it?'

'If you don't, my reputation will be in

pieces,' the surgeon replied quietly. 'You have little to fear; I have operated with considerable success so far. Of course, there is always . . . '

'If there's the slightest doubt about my recovery I feel I ought to confide in you the details of a discovery I have made, in order that my secret may not be lost to the world.'

'Certainly there is always a risk,' the brain specialist admitted. 'Why not confide in me in any case? We're old friends. You can tell me anything with absolute confidence; I won't breathe a word to a soul.'

'I know,' Downing nodded, simply — in fact, too simply. Even through ten years of close acquaintance he had not fully pierced that strange diverse and even treacherous inner nature of his medical friend. Doctor Adam Henderson was not all he seemed on the surface; a streak of cruelty, and an inveterate desire for gambling, had more than once threatened to undermine his career. Only his amazing brilliance and the utilization of an alias had kept him at the pinnacle of fame as a brain-surgeon.

Downing was a different type. Quiet, unassuming, oblivious to all glory, his main object in life the exploration into little known science. He had already amassed a considerable fortune by the medium of his inventions. Henderson, always in the hope that something would be discovered that would perhaps net him a fortune as well, had clung to Downing like a leech through the years — so far without any benefit . . .

'I've made a really remarkable discovery.' Downing began reminiscently, seating himself. 'I've found how to stop the action of gravitation. It's a metal — Vonium, I call it; highly radioactive.'

'So you've added another element to the Periodic Table, then? That's rather out of my line, Downing. I know little of radioactive minerals.'

'In a way, it was an accident which led me to discover it. I was endeavouring, by firing neutrons into uranium atoms — to bring about a new metal — but instead of a transmutation into some new and inert metal, I brought about a substance, which instantly flew to the top of the vacuum-tube in which I was making the experiment! The top, mind you! The substance proved to be extremely radio-active, and in due course turned back into uranium. Once that happened it fell again to the base of the vacuum-tube.'

'Well?' Henderson asked, as a momentary silence settled on the inventor.

'I repeated the experiment and made a thorough investigation, finally arriving at the cause of this peculiar defiance of gravitation . . . You've heard of radiation?'

'Who hasn't?'

'I mean, do you really understand its relationship to radioactivity? For instance, all radioactive substances emit radiation in the form of y-rays, and material particles in the form of alpha and beta rays are shot off, these latter being, of course, the protons and electrons of the original atom. Now, y-rays are not material particles; they're merely radiation of a very special kind. Note the word 'radiation' Henderson, for that is the secret. Radiation from a normally radio-active substance is amazingly weak, of course, its wavelength being about the order of one ten thousand millionth of an inch, or about the hundred thousandth part of the wavelength of visible light.'

'Figures don't impress me, Downing; I like visible proof.'

'Wait a minute; I have to explain it this way. I have shown how weak normal radiation is; yet even so that radiation had been proved by various scientists to possess a faint recoiling power; that is to say it has a slight, measurable mass, just as has light itself in a stronger form. This new element has a diffusion of energy that exceeds anything hitherto known to science. The radiation of the y-rays is strong enough to actually repulse the metal itself against the power of gravitation. You understand?'

The surgeon's pale eyes were brighter now. 'I see what you mean. Radioactivity is so extremely rapid that the y-rays are emitted with infinitely greater power than in a normal radioactive substance, causing the metal concerned to recede under its own power from gravitational force?'

'There you have it in a nutshell. Of

course, extreme radioactivity of that kind limits the life of Vonium to one of extreme shortness; its weight vanishes as radiation goes on, naturally — that is law. Then it returns to the original element, uranium.'

'But surely, if the stuff is such a repulsor of gravitation, it would hang in the middle of the tube, not at the top, by reason of it exerting an equal repulsive pressure on all sides?'

'It would seem natural at first thought,' Downing agreed, 'but you must not forget that the mass of the vacuum walls, as compared to the mass of the earth — the floor — is immeasurably slight. Vonium releases itself from the strongest attraction, which is earth itself; hence it goes upward until it meets the first obstacle — in this case the top of the vacuum-tube. I haven't tried releasing it yet. I suppose it would go into space in a perfectly straight line so long as its life lasted — except where it repulsed itself from stellar bodies. One thing I do know; it won't stop down!'

'It sounds too remarkable to be true,' the surgeon said thoughtfully. 'I wish I knew more of atomic science.'

'So far, the world has never known a substance which can repulse itself by its own radiations, but that doesn't preclude its existence. I've found it. Energy and radiation are one and the same, Henderson. Anything that goes forward has a thrust backwards — recoil.'

'And now what?' Henderson asked. 'Space travel, I suppose?'

The inventor shook his head. 'Not to commence with. There are thousands of other uses for the stuff, here on earth — such as in the erection of high buildings. Once I've got the stuff under proper control men can have boots made of the stuff, within lead-casings because of the harmful radiations, and then they can walk literally on air. Calculation will show when the stuff will revert back to inert metal . . . There are cranes, too, which can be replaced with Vonium. Sufficient quantities will lift any weight on earth. Uranium isn't particularly difficult to secure these days, and the transmutation task is fairly simple. I'm sure boots are the simplest things to begin with.'

'I'd like to see how you do all this,' Henderson remarked, and at that Downing rose to his feet.

'You shall. It's essential you should know what to do in case anything happens to me. Come into the lab.'

For nearly two hours the pale-eyed surgeon watched, mutely, the transmutation of uranium into Vonium. Unaccustomed to this branch of science, the giant vacuum tube in which the stuff was created, the humming of power, and the glowing electrodes and numberless electrical contacts held him fascinated.

'There it is!' Downing exclaimed at last, and pointed to the newly-created metal, visibly glowing, pressed immovably against the upper walls of the vacuum-tube. 'Tomorrow I shall devise how to make boots.'

'And what of your operation?' the surgeon asked presently. 'How long did the specialist give you?'

'A week at the most.' The inventor smiled dryly. 'I can do a lot in a week, my friend — and then I shall entrust my body and brain to your capable hands. Between that time and now I will find how to harness Vonium and will write down a full formula, just in case anything happens to me. If anything goes wrong with me — you are to use and perfect the invention. You understand?'

'Yes,' Henderson said, and looked away into the tube. He felt unable to meet his friend's steady grey eyes.

'I'm not leaving you a white elephant,' Downing resumed presently, as he switched off the various power-machines. 'Three representatives of the Federated Alliance Engineering were here yesterday; they saw the possibilities of Vonium and offered me twenty million dollars for the formula. Naturally I turned it down.'

'You turned down twenty million dollars!' the surgeon breathed dazedly.

'Yes, because it is worth at least three times as much . . . Still, the offer was made, and I suppose it is still open for anybody who takes Federated the formula — thieves included! If the invention should fall into your hands, don't let Federated have it for anything less than sixty million. Improve on it first. Promise me that!'

'I'll do what I think is wisest, Downing — be assured of that.'

'All right,' the inventor smiled. 'And now, if you'll pardon me, I must get on with my work. Don't think me discourteous, but — '

'I quite understand, Downing; I'll be getting along. When anything important turns up let me know right away. I'll keep a date open for your operation . . . '

'Splendid. Goodbye, Henderson.'

Doctor Henderson returned to his home to find a visitor waiting. Grumbling to himself at the presence, presumably, of a patient at so late an hour, he gave instructions for him to be sent into the surgery.

'Good evening, Doctor,' was the visitor's greeting, and there was a hint of menace in his tone. Henderson looked up with a start; he knew the voice. When he beheld the man's face he realised that he had seen it before, and not under pleasant conditions, either.

'So it's you Holroyd!' Henderson

126

murmured, essaying affability. 'Well, what can I do for you? What's your ailment?'

'The lack of one hundred thousand dollars, Doctor,' Holroyd answered grimly. 'I've given you three opportunities to pay that sum, money which you owe me on gambling losses, and so far you've ignored me. I'm a just man, Henderson; I've refrained so far from ruining your reputation, but I'm not standing for it much longer. See?'

'Meaning what?' The surgeon's pale eyes were malignant.

'Pay me the sum you owe — within fourteen days — or else I'll expose you. It won't look pretty, Henderson! World's greatest brain surgeon's double life — gambling under an alias; owing enormous sums to various people. Known to every gaming house, under a different assumed name each time!'

'You're a fool. My private life won't affect my profession. I shall still be the world's greatest surgeon!'

'Yes?' Holroyd sneered. 'You do other things besides gamble, Doctor. Drinking for instance. Oh. I know you take powerful emetics to rid yourself of the stuff before you ever attempt a case, but who's going to trust themselves again under your knife, knowing that?'

'And where do you expect I'll get one hundred thousand?' Henderson snapped. 'Even to a man of my position that is a considerable sum.'

'I don't care where you get it — but do it in fourteen days. Either pay me or I'll revenge myself. The latter course won't pay my debts for me, of course, but will appease me somewhat Goodnight!'

Henderson blinked as the surgery door slammed; he bit his thin underlip slowly. 'One hundred thousand dollars! I knew that blow would fall sooner or later — and I've got to find it, too! And to think that that fool Downing turns down twenty million for the love of his art. Twenty millions! By heaven, I just wonder . . . ' He paused, lighted a cigar and gave himself up to meditation . . .

Three days later Henderson was summoned by an urgent phone call to Downing's home. He found the inventor jubilant when he joined him in his laboratory.

'Well, Henderson, I've done it!' Downing pointed to a pair of military trench-boots, possessing enormously thick soles of lead.

In the leg-part of each boot reposed a small dial face, marked from zero to maximum, whilst a delicate needle pointed to the latter reading. In each heel there appeared to be a small electric motor, connected to the boot-soles by wires, and controlled by long cables lying, at the moment, on the floor and terminating in hand sprocket-levers.

Quietly Henderson studied these details. The thought of twenty million dollars was in his brain; then he looked up.

'Well, they seem all right,' he said perfunctorily. 'What have you done?'

'First I created Vonium as usual, but equipped my tube with a slide on the top so that the stuff could be released when made. Over the gap left by the moving slide I placed a box of lead, bottomless, and not unnaturally the stuff shot into it. I had, however, created a quantity large enough to lift me into the air, with the result that I would have been jerked to the ceiling had I not released my hold. The stuff hit the ceiling and stopped there, inside the lead box. Then arose the problem of how to control the stuff, which I solved by a remarkably simple means.

'The y-rays of Vonium, those responsible for this curious non-gravitational effect, are blocked entirely by sufficient thickness of lead and the stuff instantly falls to the ground. It appears, though, that when this happens, the Vonium inside the box fixes itself in the dead centre of the box, equally repulsed from all four side walls. See?'

Henderson nodded. 'What then?'

'I fixed a lead sheath on the bottom of the box — by the simple expedient of standing on step ladders and reaching up to it — and when this was done, the y-rays cut off, the box dropped to the floor. From then on it was only a matter of fixing the lead sheath base so that all or little of the y-radiations could be emitted at will. I accomplished this by means of a shutter and a small electric motor attached to the side of the box. Later I made two motors and put them in the heels of those boots there, and two boxes also which I rivetted to the boot-soles. From the motors I lead the contact wires, at the end of which, held in the hand — one hand for one boot — are notched levers, which move the shutters in the sole-boxes. Naturally, the more radiations there are being emitted the higher you'll go. When you've reached a certain height you'll stay in mid-air. Then you can walk about in the air at that height. Close the shutter very slowly, and down you come to earth again. Very simple and efficient.'

'Apparently so,' Henderson agreed, 'but I don't quite see how you balance in the air. What is to prevent you turning circles round a kind of central axis — the boots?'

'The lead plays a three-fold part. One, it controls the power of the y-rays; two, it stops them entering the flesh and mortifying it, and three, its enormous weight keeps the body upright, just as do divers' boots. In air one is like a ship with a heavy keel — quite impossible to turn turtle.'

Downing crossed over to the boots and began putting them on. 'I'll demonstrate to you.'

Before he laced them he pointed to the two small dials in the leg portions.

'These show when the Vonium is losing its efficiency and therefore is no longer safe,' he explained. 'A very necessary attachment. It would be rather awkward to be five hundred feet up and find the Vonium giving out. As Vonium loses its weight by radiation, these meters here show, on the principle of a spring balance, when the weight of Vonium inside the boxes has touched zero. That means replace with more Vonium, of course. At the moment, as you see, there is a considerable amount of life left in the present charge of Vonium — enough for a few weeks, anyhow. However, here's the demonstration.'

Downing quickly laced the boots up, stood up, and grasped the control-levers of the heavily insulated wires leading to the motors controlling the sole-shutters.

'Watch!' he bade impressively, and gently pressed the pincer-like levers towards each other, in either hand. Almost instantly he began to rise smoothly and irresistibly towards the high laboratory roof, pausing finally in mid-air 'twixt ceiling and floor, the notched levers fixing themsclves in the small ratchets provided for the purpose. Then, without hardly any trace of clumsiness, he began to walk forward, albeit ponderously, but none the less certainly.

Doctor Henderson stood gazing upwards, astounded at the uncanny aspect his friend presented,

For a while Downing continued his mid-air stroll, then, lowering himself to the floor, he opened the laboratory door and went outside on the lawn. Five minutes later hc was on a level with the treetop, presently alighting on the flat roof of his home close to thc bedroom window of his manservant, Dawson.

Laughing, he returned to the ground.

'Achievement number one,' he chuck-led, unlacing the boots. Later will come the construction of super-cranes, space travel — hundreds of things. Boots like these can be made for workmen on high buildings, thereby dispensing with ladders and clumsy, dangerous scaffoldings. Here.' he wrenched the boots off — 'you try them.'

Rather gingerly Henderson put them on, and after one or two unsuccessful efforts, managed to get them under control. He found the air apparently as solid as the ground, and as he went around, accustoming himself, the thought of twenty million dollars rose up and stared him in the face.

At length he returned to earth, both in the literal and abstract sense.

'Suppose one opened the shutters to their fullest extent?' he asked, unlacing the boots.

'In that case one would shoot upwards into space, never to return,' Downing replied. 'That won't happen though; I've fixed the levers so they can't operate to the full . . . Come along into the lab; I've something to tell you.'

Henderson replaced his shoes and obeyed, carrying the heavy boots with him.

'I'm giving those boots to you for the time being,' Downing said quietly. 'Until after my operation — which God grant I survive — I'm doing no more work, and in case anything happens to me I want you to keep those boots so you can see how they work.'

'Thanks,' the surgeon said, his mind active.

'I've written out the formula for Vonium in invisible ink and also the method of its manufacture, and full directions of how to harness it. The formula itself is inside a massive gold watch, and the watch is in that safe there, on the wall. Heat will bring the invisible ink into view. I have also made a will with my lawyer, which, in the event of my death, bequeaths everything to you. Should you at any time wish to withdraw yourself from the bequest, everything passes to my brother Walter, who is an Australian farmer . . . The safe there has a combination lock, and Dawson is the only one outside me who knows that combination.'

'Dawson!' Henderson started. 'You're letting your manservant in on this?'

'He's something more than that — he is, I think, a devoted friend. In withholding the safe combination from you I'm protecting you. Should anything happen to me as the result of your operating on me, and it became known that you knew the safe combination before you operated, it might appear that — forgive me saying this — that you killed me for the sake of the invention. If, on the other hand, you are found to be in ignorance of the combination until after my death, you'll be absolved from all blame in the eyes of the law. Understand?'

Henderson tried hard not to reveal his displeasure. He inclined his head slowly.

'Thanks for thinking of my reputation, Downing! But why the invisible ink?'

'Dawson does not know I've written the formula in invisible ink — nor does he know it is concealed inside a watch. If he chose to act unworthily, which I don't think he ever would, he'd probably pass over the watch as of no consequence — or, if he probed further and found blank paper inside it, he'd give up the task. That metal Vonium is for your hands alone if mine fail. By the plan I've outlined I'm protecting both of you.'

'And if anything happens to you I'm to

ask Dawson for the combination?'

'My lawyer will instruct Dawson to give it to you. He understands the circumstances, and will exercise law in the right direction.'

'Well, I must admit you've made things secure,' Henderson remarked, though he could not completely disguise the bitterness of his tone. 'Since you are ready for your operation I propose to get to work on you tomorrow morning. Be at my home tonight by seven, ready for the preliminaries. I will notify my assistants and have everything in readiness. Naturally, I shall operate on you in my own private theatre, not at the hospital.'

'Seven tonight, then, my friend,' Downing said quietly. 'If I die — you must go on.'

'Yes — you have already made that very clear to me. Goodbye till tonight, Downing — and thanks for the boots!'

Henderson picked them up and slowly left the laboratory, his thoughts by no means of the sweetest . . .

Towards late afternoon, after a day's hard medical work, Doctor Henderson returned for a brief space to his library. He was surprised to find Dawson, Downing's manservant, awaiting him. He rose to his feet, as compact and composed as ever.

'Pardon my intrusion, Doctor. But I have something of considerable importance to say to you, regarding my master's brain operation.'

'Well, Dawson?'

'If you killed him, entirely by circumstances beyond your control, of course — you would be the sole owner of Vonium — by the terms of his will, which I personally witnessed, would you not?'

'How dare you presume to question my ability, Dawson?' Henderson snapped. 'If I fail, I fail — it cannot be helped.'

'It would be to your advantage to fail,' said Dawson calmly, never moving a muscle of his saturnine countenance.

'Why, you impudent . . .'

'It would mean you could pay off the one hundred thousand dollars you owe and so save at least one possible destroyer of your reputation, wouldn't it?'

'How in hell do you know my private

affairs?' Henderson grated out, glaring.

'Albert Holroyd, the man to whom you owe that sum, happens to be my cousin,' the manservant replied, and smiled winterily. 'He needs that money badly; quite recently, in the strictest confidence of course, he told me all about you, and about the terms he made with you. But I warn you, Doctor, that my master's life had better not be the means for you to pay your debts! If, by a — shall we say — professional error? — you kill my master, I will kill you. I hope you understand, sir?'

'And go to the chair for it!' Henderson retorted curtly.

'Oh, no, I am not such a fool, Doctor. I could provide an explanation by outlining your financial difficulties; add to that the worry at killing your devoted friend, which you believed had completely shattered your reputation, and provide suicide as the motive. If you take Mr. Downing's life, you can count yours as ended too — whether you kill him fortuitously, or otherwise. I know it won't be an accident, because you have never made an error yet!'

'The human element can always err,' Henderson panted; then cooling again, 'Does Downing know you've come here?'

'No, sir; he imagines I'm posting an urgent letter to an ailing aunt of mine. Anyhow, please bear in mind what I've said. Of course, if you fail and do kill my master your reputation will probably be spoilt in any case; on the other hand that very failure would place a considerable amount of money in your hands, which would make failure well worthwhile. Don't do it, Doctor — you might find it unpleasant afterwards.'

'Get out of here!' Henderson breathed dangerously. 'Get out — before I 'phone Mr. Downing and tell him everything.'

'How very droll, Doctor. You won't do that, it would ruin your own plans. Good day, sir — and don't forget!'

The library door closed and Henderson sank down into his chair. He admitted now, quite frankly, that he had intended killing Downing by a slip of the knife, but now that scheme was quashed. Confound Dawson having Holroyd for a cousin!

Downing's invention and at least twenty million dollars on the one hand, but courting death to get it. Disgrace and ruin on the other hand if Downing lived . . .

Adam Henderson had reason to be worried — but as time passed another scheme formulated in his fertile brain.

When finally he left the library there was a smile on his face, a smile of frozen hardness . . .

By nine o'clock that same evening, Jarvis Downing was sleeping heavily beneath a narcotic; no ordinary narcotic, but a substance of Henderson's own invention, capable of reducing the animation of the body to absolute zero by slow degrees, producing complete coldness and apparent death, and at the same time hardening the crystals of the blood so that no bleeding could possibly occur during the actual operation. Then, under the administration of an antidote, after the operation, the patient would return with like slowness to life . . .

Henderson stood for a while looking at his sleeping friend.

'You shan't die, Downing,' he murmured to himself. 'That would endanger me — but indeed it is good fortune that your brain tumour happens to be on the right frontal lobe. If I make a professional mistake I shan't kill you; I shall merely destroy every vestige of your memory. The right lobe has no connection with muscular functions, but is entirely connected with the storage of memory impressions. How inconvenient for you if I remove certain cells, along with the tumour, and so destroy your memory but not your powers of perception and conception.'

The surgeon ceased his soliloquy, smiled significantly to himself, and quietly left the bedroom . . . He spent the night making his preparations; he felt he could not sleep, and at nine the next morning the operation commenced in the private theatre, with only a few trusted assistants.

They said nothing — indeed they did not understand enough — as they watched their master at work. His hands were steady; he wielded his instruments with the deft skill that had earned him his name, and when finally he washed his hands in antiseptic that same frozen smile of complacency had returned to his thin lips.

'Simple,' he murmured; then went into the adjoining room where Downing was lying, bandaged and still unconscious. At frequent intervals thereafter he returned, dismissing the nurse each time, until towards ten in the evening the inventor revealed signs of returning consciousness. The surgeon took a rapid diagnosis of his bodily functions, and found him as healthy as could be expected in the circumstances, but — Jarvis Downing was a man entirely without memory. Everything he had ever known or learned had been completely effaced — as though he were born again as an adult man. He looked at Henderson with an empty, vacant stare.

A week later he was able to sit up, but still unable to even speak. Everything would have to be taught to him all over again. Even food had to be taken by the nurse, in pantomime, to show what was required of him . . .

Dawson arrived on one of the days and compressed his lips when the result of the operation was made clear to him. Grimly, the nurse being once more dismissed, he looked across Downing's supine body at the surgeon.

'Well, what do you expect to gain by this?' he demanded coldly. 'You have spared his life, but returned him to the state of a new-born baby. I can't touch you now because you've destroyed my alibi. What's your motive in this fiendish scheme?'

'There is a clause in law, Dawson, that relegates a person of mental deficiency, to the same class as that of a deceased. Downing is dead to the law; his identity has vanished, and any lawyer on earth will support me. Vonium is my property once I have seen Downing's lawyer, and you will be required to hand over the formula. In fact you've retained it unlawfully as it is; you've known your master's condition for some days. Hand it to me now, and I'll see to it that the law leaves you alone — otherwise you will be summoned for unlawful retention of my property.'

Dawson's urbanity vanished; a bitter smile curved his lips.

'A clever trick, Henderson — you think I know nothing of the law, eh? I know quite as much as you do — enough to realise, anyhow, that a will only becomes operative on decease. Naturally you planned to bribe the lawyer, I suppose. It might have worked, too — men will do anything for money, as a rule. It so happens, though, that I'm leaving this safe combination just where it is — in my wallet. And, if I can prove anything against you I'm going to, and take over Vonium myself!'

'You dare — ' Henderson breathed venomously.

'I probably will,' the manservant answered calmly, passed another glance at the silent man in the bed, and then left the room . . .

For the remainder of the day after Dawson's departure, Henderson spent the time thinking, leaving Downing in the charge of the nurse, ignoring, so far as he could, all cases that came to his surgery. In seven days, now, he had got to produce one hundred thousand dollars. Further, the determined Dawson might find a way to prove Downing's condition to be the outcome of deliberate maltreatment.

Why not kill Dawson? No, that would probably raise enquiry.

The desperate surgeon knew his last card had failed. He had hoped that Dawson would have been ignorant of the law; unfortunately, he wasn't. Presently Henderson recalled the manservant's words to the effect that the safe combination was in his wallet. Steal it? It would be quieter than bringing in a third party to crack the safe open, anyhow. Suppose, by an accident, that Dawson did die? He — Henderson — would be eternally safe from then onwards. The recollection of the gravity-nullifying boots returned to the surgeon. At least the manservant knew nothing of these. They might be very useful.

Finally, Henderson had a plan in mind, and the thought of expulsion from his profession, or Dawson finding proof to convict him, was undoubtedly the prime motive behind it.

At eight o'clock he put on the gravity-boots, slipped a loaded revolver and diamond glass-cutter and suction-cup in his pocket, then with clumsy steps made his way to Downing's room, curtly dismissing the nurse, but taking care she did not see his feet as she departed.

Downing looked at Henderson dully, mutely. He for his part pulled on washleather gloves, then, without uttering a word wrapped the inventor in two heavy blankets, raised him bodily in his arms, and finally managed to get the bemused man to link his arms round his — Henderson's — neck, thereby leaving the surgeon free to use his hands.

This done the surgeon quietly lifted the window sash and climbed on to the sill, Downing clinging tightly to him. The hand-levers clicked in their sprockets, and in a few moments Henderson was walking in the air twenty feet above the night-ridden lawn below, making allowance as he went for the inventor's extra weight. He walked on steadily through space, over the solitary window-lighted patch of Benton's Farm, across the intervening meadows, and finally came within sight of the inventor's own home, dimly visible in the starlight. Ten minutes later he had reached it, and laid Downing down gently on the flat roof. The dazed man made no effort to move; indeed it was doubtful if he understood the first principles of locomotion. He merely pulled the blankets further round him and sat as still as a mummy.

In utter silence, thanks to the emptiness in which he walked, Henderson moved along the bedroom windows until he came to the one that he knew to be Dawson's, at a height of a sheer thirty feet from the ground. The manservant might be downstairs, of course or even out. Considering the valuable apparatus in the house the latter theory was hardly tenable . . . No — he was in bed, dimly visible in the starlight. Henderson could clearly see that now, for the curtains were not drawn.

With infinite care he brought out the diamond glass-cutter and suction cup from his pocket. In the space of a few minutes he had removed a section of the window glass, felt inside for and slipped back the catch, and then, carefully operating his hand-levers, climbed into the room beyond, keeping himself a bare couple of inches from the floor to negate all sound.

The manservant's clothes were neatly spread at the end of the bed, and towards them the surgeon moved.

Be it said to his credit that he did not intend to use his revolver if he could avoid it -- it was only a precautionary measure, that would need Downing to substantiate the motive. The precaution, however, changed abruptly to dire necessity as Dawson suddenly awoke — indeed it was doubtful if he had ever been asleep — and his revolver, which manifestly had been close to his hand, blazed through the gloomy room.

Instantly, the manservant's shot flying wide, Henderson swung round, whipped out his own weapon, and emptied all the chambers with ruthless deliberation into the already advancing manservant. He staggered, gave a short cry, and then fell his length to the floor.

Carefully, still completely cool, the

surgeon went through the man's clothes, finally located the wallet and the combination for the safe within it. Chuckling to himself he slipped the wallet in his pocket, and made an investigation of the sprawling Dawson. The briefest examination revealed to his professional touch that the man was quite dead, and bleeding somewhat considerably.

Rising again, his Vonium boots now temporarily out of action, he left the room and entered the next but one. Outside the window he found the still motionless Downing, lifted him inside, and carried him by main strength to the dead servant's room, depositing him on the bed. Still without speaking, for he knew the inventor would never understand, he placed the expended revolver in the motionless Downing's limp hand, taking care he still wore his gloves whilst he did so. Then, after a final glance round the room, he again departed locking the door on the outside, and went as fast as his heavy boots would allow him to the laboratory safe.

It was the work of a moment to open

the heavy door and remove the gold watch. Sure enough the formula was inside it.

Henderson grinned as he slipped the watch in his pocket.

'Really very simple,' he murmured. 'All a matter of judgment and precision.'

He did not return upstairs to the silent inventor. He left the laboratory, once assured that everything was as he had found it, and went by various air-routes to the nearest telephone kiosk. In a few moments he was speaking to the head-warder of the local asylum.

'Doctor Henderson speaking,' he announced, in his calm voice. 'I operated quite recently on a patient, Jarvis Downing by name. He had brain trouble and seemed to be progressing quite well until tonight. Then I found he had vanished from his room at my home, taking with him my own revolver from my study. I've proved that fact right up to the hilt. However, I've traced him to his old home and he has murdered his manservant — filled the poor devil with lead. He's clean homicidal. I think he had a grudge against his manservant, or something. Anyhow, I've locked him in the manservant's room, complete with revolver. His memory seems to have gone utterly; doesn't say anything or hear anything apparently. You'd better drop along and take him away at once. I'll join you there. The Larches, Menison Road, is the address.'

'We'll be there, Doctor,' the head-warder answered firmly, and with a grin of triumph Henderson hung up the receiver and left the kiosk. Outside he ruminated for a moment, patting the gold watch in his pocket.

'A clear twenty million for me tomorrow when I sell this formula to Federated; Dawson out of the way so he can't prove anything against me; Holroyd paid up, and Downing no longer at liberty. Then a life of ease — and I've earned it. Monte-Carlo — the gaming tables . . . Yes — a good night's work. I've just time to get home and be rid of these boots, make a substantiating tale for the nurse, and everything is settled. Splendid! I'll be back in plenty of time for the asylum men.'

Again smiling to himself at his work, he seized the boot-levers and moved upwards into the darkness of the night, turning towards his own home to the south . . .

For some then strange reason the men from the asylum found Doctor Henderson absent when they arrived at Downing's home. Finally, obtaining no answer, they took the law into their own hands and broke in, arriving ultimately at the locked bedroom door. This too they smashed down, to discover Downing still sitting there, completely silent, the revolver still in his hand.

'That's him, all right,' nodded the superintendent. 'Take him away; I'll notify the police about this body.' He looked at Downing closely. 'Why don't you say something?' he demanded curtly, and for a space tried every means he could devise to make the inventor speak, without success. Finally he waved him away.

'O.K. — he's our man all right. Guess Henderson got him in here pretty safe, too — couldn't leave by the window with a thirty-foot drop below. Yet he got in by the window — see the glass is cut out. Guess he must have walked along that parapet there. Funny what a guy'll do when he's deranged ... Queer where Henderson's got to. Still he'll turn up to verify things, I suppose.'

But Doctor Henderson did not turn up. Nobody could discover what had become of him. Downing was duly removed to the asylum and placed under the care of the institution's medical expert, who gravely pronounced that only one man could possibly cure him — and that was Doctor Henderson himself. It was accepted without question that Downing had committed the crime of murder — truly not whilst responsible for his actions. All the efforts of the inventor's lawyer to prove otherwise — to try and prove the vanished Henderson to be the culprit, failed. The law coldly bequeathed Downing's home and invention to his disinterested brother Walter, who, rather than give up his prosperous Australian farm, allowed his inheritance to go to rack and ruin.

Poor Downing — He was ruined

utterly — mentally, physically and financially. As week followed week he was gradually taught to do various things, but gone forever was the brilliance that had once been his.

And Henderson? A month after Downing's admittance to the asylum the surgeon was found — stone dead! It appeared that Oscar Benton, who owned the farm between the homes of Henderson and Downing, had returned with his family after a brief holiday in the metropolis, and the farmer had been horrified to discover Henderson lying transfixed, nearly buried in mud — which probably accounted for the failure of search-parties to discover him — with a six-foot iron spike through his abdomen. The spike was the corner support of a net-fencing for the chicken run. It had passed slantwise through Henderson's body, even passing through a gold watch he had had in his pocket, crushing to pulp some insignificant blank white paper within. Upon his feet were peculiar boots, and in his death-frozen hands reposed queer levers.

The world duly mourned the death of the great brain-surgeon, and Downing's chances of recovery were simultaneously shattered. But there were many who wondered how on earth the surgeon had come to meet such a terrible yet peculiar death. How had he come to impale himself on a six-foot high spike, and with such force?

But then, how was the world to know that, in his excitement to get home with the Vonium formula, Henderson had forgotten to look at the radiation-registers on his boots. They had registered almost zero — the Vonium had practically transformed itself back during the passing days into lifeless uranium — hence the surgeon had been in mid-air when the stuff had suddenly come to the end of its life, dropping him down — with tremendous speed owing to the weight of the heavy lead boots and equally heavy uranium — to instant death!

Part 4

Alice, Where Art Thou?

1

This is the strange story of Alice Denham, whom I should have married ten years ago but did not. At the time, as some of the older amongst you will remember, there was quite a stir when Alice disappeared. I was even very close to being accused of her murder, along with Dr Earl Page. The only reason we escaped was because no trace could be found of Alice's body — and according to law, no body — no accusation. Instead the case of Alice became relegated to one of those 'peculiar' stories, such as footprints mysteriously ceasing to advance through unbroken snow.

I did not give the real facts concerning Alice ten years ago because I knew I would never be believed, nor Dr Page either. The thing was — and still is — so incredible. And yet it happened.

Suppose we go back to the beginning? My name is Rodney Fletcher. Ten years ago I had just started business on my own as a stockbroker and had every prospect of a successful business career. Today I am comparatively well-to-do, but still unmarried. There can never be anybody to take the place of Alice, so far as I am concerned.

It was just after I had set up in business that I first met Alice. She was a slim, elfin-type of girl with a wealth of blonde hair, smoke-gray eyes, and a tremendous amount of enthusiasm. She first came sailing into my orbit when I advertised for a secretary-receptionist. I had little hesitation over engaging her and in the space of a year she had become the supervisor of my ever-increasing clerical staff.

Inevitably I was drawn to her, and she to me. We exchanged confidences, we dined together. Our friendship deepened into romance; then one warm spring evening at twilight, as we were strolling through the city to keep a theatre date together, we decided to become engaged.

At the time of this decision, which did not come as a surprise to either of us, we were just passing the brilliantly lighted window of a famous city jeweller's. I think it was the sight of a certain ring that prompted the abrupt decision to become engaged.

That certain ring! If only to God we'd never seen it! If only we had taken another street . . . but of what avail now to try to turn back the clock? There the ring was — compelling, seeming even to beckon us to look at it. We even forgot for the moment that we had decided to become engaged. Fixedly we looked at that ring. We wondered about it. We exchanged glances of awe.

The ring had been cunningly placed in the centre of the resplendent window so that it automatically attracted the eye. Around it were grouped trays of diamond rings, together with pendants of sapphires, rubies, opals, and all the stock in trade of a high-class jeweler. The shop was still open and within, when at last we managed to drag our eyes from the ring, we could see a glimpse of an elderly man silently writing something in a ledger.

'Did you *ever* see anything like it, Rod?'

Alice's gentle, fascinated voice brought my attention back to the ring. The circlet holding the stone was normal enough and made of platinum, but the stone itself was as large as a small pea and radiated colors in a fashion neither of us had ever seen before. From the countless facets there flooded a blazing emerald green one moment, or ruby-red the next. We had only to move position by a fraction of an inch and the color changed again. Once even it seemed to me that there were faint glimpses of colors not within the normal spectrum, colors, which one sensed rather than saw. Yet how am I to describe a colour that has no normal parallel? By and large, the stone looked as though it were a composite of all precious gems rolled into one. Quite definitely, neither of us had ever seen anything like it.

And we had just become engaged. Was there anything illogical in the fact that we finally turned into the shop and asked to see the masterpiece at close quarters?

'Ah, yes — the Sunstone,' the jeweller said, smiling, and put aside his ledger. 'Quite a remarkable gem . . . '

He opened the barred cage-work at the back of the window and with exquisite care lifted the ring, complete on its plush display case. Still very gently he set it down on the glass-topped counter before us. And all Alice and I could do was stare at it, just as though it possessed some incredible hypnotic quality.

It had no such powers of course; it was simply that the unearthly, blazing luster held the eye with a magnetism all their own.

'A wonderful, wonderful stone,' came the jeweler's voice, and at that I forced myself to look at him. He was an intellectual-looking man of late middle-age, with thick white hair curling at his temples.

'Where did it come from?' I asked. 'I don't think I ever saw anything like it!'

'To the best of my knowledge, sir, and I have checked very carefully, it is the only specimen of its kind in the world. It was found originally in South America, became a sacred gem to a race now long forgotten, and eventually fell into the hands of an explorer. After that it travelled considerably, leaving quite a history everywhere it went.'

'A history?' Alice questioned. 'What sort of history, apart from its natural beauty?'

'A history which I find very hard to credit, madam,' the jeweller smiled. 'Or perhaps that is because I am too mature to be gullible. It *does* appear, though, that every owner of this ring up to now has vanished.'

'Oh?' Alice looked surprised. 'Vanished? To where?'

'That is what is so strange. Nobody seems to know. The ring has remained, but the various owners have disappeared — nor have they ever been traced . . . Of course,' the jeweler continued, perhaps realizing he was jeopardizing his chance of a sale, 'it may all be a lot of nonsense — and probably is. Just superstitious gossip, such as often does attach to a gem of unusual qualities. However, through various trade processes it finally came into my possession, and I am glad to say that in the two months I have possessed it I have not disappeared!'

Somehow it was a relief to laugh. And the ring still blazed up at us from its deep amethyst plush case . . . After a moment Alice withdrew her glove and reached a pale, slender hand tentatively forward.

'May I?' she questioned, and the jeweler quietly pushed the case towards her.

'By all means, madam. I have never yet seen how it looks on the finger of a woman.'

With my help Alice slid the ring experimentally on the third finger of her right hand.

Then she held her hand forward and turned it back and forth so the ring caught the lights. And the effect was breathtaking. It looked exactly as though sheer emerald and ruby fire were burning her finger away.

'Exquisite! Exquisite!' This seemed to be the only word she could whisper.

'But on the wrong finger,' I smiled.

'So — an engagement?' the jeweller asked. 'I do congratulate you. I am sure no other woman will ever possess so exquisite an engagement ring, madam.'

Alice looked a little embarrassed, gently eased the ring from her finger, and put it back in the case. The jeweller waited, apparently sensing by some business instinct that he had made a sale even though the ring was back where it had started.

'It must be frightfully expensive,' Alice said, and at that I imagine I looked indignant. Certainly I felt it.

'Who cares about that? I don't want the woman I love to wear *any* sort of trash . . . What *is* the figure?' I turned to the jeweller.

'As rings go it is not expensive, sir. Besides, its odd history, be it true or false, forbids a high figure . . . The price is ten thousand pounds.'

I suppose that should have been a shock, but it was not. I mentally decided that should the need arise — which I considered highly unlikely — I would be more than able to get my money back by selling the ring. One always has to pay to be unique, so I made out my cheque there and then and handed it over. My business card was sufficient guarantee to the jeweller that I was a man of standing — and so we departed. Alice and I, she with the ring now on the third finger of her left hand and her smile one of ecstatic satisfaction.

'I shall never forget this evening as long as I live,' she murmured, as we went on our way to the theatre. 'Engaged, and the possessor of the most wonderful ring in the world — all in one fell swoop.'

'Nothing but the best for the best,' I told her.

So we kept our theater date, but throughout the performance our attention kept wandering to that blaze of glory on Alice's slim hand. For that matter we were not the only ones looking at it. In our position in the orchestra stall we were close enough for the foremost members of the play to see us with some distinctness. I could not help but notice the fascinated stare of the young heroine as her eye caught that shimmering grandeur below. So fascinated was she that she nearly forgot her lines!

Yes, as Alice had said, that evening was a wonderful, memorable one. As for the strange story that went with the ring, we neither of us gave it another thought. We were both supremely happy, and before I departed from Alice towards midnight we had arranged to be married within a month. There seemed to be no point in a long engagement since we both knew exactly what we intended doing . . . From this day forward she would cease to be a member of my stock broking firm and make her arrangements for the great day.

On the following morning I was at the office as usual, too many business matters on my mind to give much thought to the aptly named 'Sunstone'. I was reminded of it, however, when towards evening Alice rang me up.

'Hello, darling!' I exclaimed, delighted to hear her voice again. 'Everything fine?'

'No, Rod, not quite. That's why I'm ringing you. I'm — I'm a bit worried.'

'What about? Nothing that can't be straightened out, surely?'

'Well, I — ' The hesitation in her gentle voice puzzled me more than somewhat. 'I wonder if you could spare the time to come over? There's something happened that's — that's not quite as it should be.'

'Spare the time!' I echoed. 'Nothing

could keep me away. I'll come immediately.'

Which I did. And I was inwardly shocked to find Alice's small, elfin-like face looking very pale and pinched. She seemed to have lost a great deal of her normal pink-and-white colour. As I stood looking at her I was seized with the curious conviction that she appeared far more frail and small than ever before. Never a big woman at anytime, she seemed definitely to have lost proportions overnight! Ridiculous, of course! Probably the light, or something.

'What is it?' I asked her quietly.

She sank down on the divan and did not speak for a moment — then with a little touch of the dramatic she held out her left hand and shook it. Immediately the amazing ring on her third finger fell to the floor and lay blazing on the carpet. I stood there and just stared for a moment or two.

'How did you *do* that?' I demanded abruptly. 'You just shook it off! That isn't possible, Alice. Last night, in the jeweller's, it only just fitted you.'

'I know, Rod. It seems to have expanded, or something.'

Alice gave me a queer look. Stooping, I picked the ring from the carpet and tested it on the end of my little finger. I had done the same thing the previous evening before giving it to her. The ring had not expanded in the least! A curious thought began to snake through my brain.

Catching at her slim hand I stared at it. I could have sworn it was far more slender and whiter than ever before.

'Alice!' I looked at her intently. 'Alice, what's wrong?'

She shook her head. 'How should I know? I seem to have lost weight and size overnight! I've been wearing this ring ever since you put it on my finger and — well, you've seen for yourself how slackly it fits.' She gave a shrug and looked at me with hollow eyes.

'Oh, what's the use of trying to disguise it, Rod? My clothes don't fit as well as they did yesterday. I've lost size in many ways. Even this belt about my dress is a notch further in than usual!'

Still I gazed at her, totally unable to

figure the business out. I said, 'It's impossible!' without realizing that I had said it.

To this Alice made no comment; then coming to a sudden decision I took Alice's arm and had her stand over by the wall.

'Flatten yourself against it,' I ordered. 'I'm going to check up. What height is recorded on your Civil Registration Card?'

She nodded to the bureau. 'Top shelf — left pigeon hole.' In a moment or two I had the card out. Here, for once, the new law to register the dimensions, size, fingerprints, and so forth of every citizen was going to prove useful. It gave Alice's height at five feet two inches, and her weight as seven and a half stones.

'Kick off your shoes,' I told her, returning to her side.

She obeyed and stood waiting. Then, with a book on top of her head and a tape measure in my hand I went to work. I made the measurement three times because I just could not believe what the measure said. She was now only five feet tall.

'Well?' she asked, as I stood thinking — and I made a quick evasion.

'Everything seems all right. What about your weight? Got a scale in the bathroom?'

She nodded and we went in to check up. Here, I had no chance to be evasive for she could see the face of the scale as well as I could. She was exactly one stone lighter in weight.

Her smoke-gray eyes were scared as she looked at me. 'Rod, what does it mean? Why have I altered like this? *Is* my height any different? For heaven's sake be frank with me!'

I put an arm about her shoulders. 'Matter of fact you're two inches shorter.'

'But why on earth should I be? What's caused it?'

'I — don't — know.' I was having a hard struggle to conceal my inward alarm. 'Something to do with the ring, perhaps. I don't think there's anything to worry about,' I added quickly. 'After all, people *do* lose weight sometimes very quickly, particularly after severe emotional strain. Maybe our getting engaged was more of a tax on your nerves than you thought.'

'That would not make me lose two inches of height, would it?'

By this time we had returned to the lounge and Alice had put her shoes on again before I had thought of an answer.

'At night, Alice, a human frame is less in height than it is in the morning because the gristle in the backbone compresses under the pull of gravity.'

'Rod, you're a very bad liar.' Alice looked at me gravely. 'You're not fooling me one little bit, you know, even though I appreciate your trying to spare my feelings. The fact remains that I am less in size in every way and I've got to know *why*!'

I picked up the ring from where I had placed ir on the occasional table. I turned it over slowly. To both of us it was no longer a thing of beauty but something to be feared and hated. Finally I wrapped it in my handkerchief and thrust it in my pocket.

'Frankly,' I confessed, 'this whole business is much too deep for me!'

'And for me! I keep thinking of the story the jeweler told us — about all the previous owners having disappeared. He didn't say in what *manner* they had disappeared, and it's sort of left me wondering . . . if . . . '

'Forget that poppycock!' I said brusquely. 'Just a lot of rubbish. Won't do you any good to brood over such stuff. Tell you what we can do. I know a Professor Earl Page, and he's a pretty good physicist. Member of the same club as I am. Just a chance this business may be scientific and that he can explain it away. Grab your hat and coat and we'll go and see. My car's outside.'

As we drove through the busy streets I reflected on the usefulness of knowing Earl Page, PhD. Though not an outstanding figure in the scientific world, he certainly knew his job when it came to scientific analysis. Indeed, his choice lay so obviously in the exploration of little known things that his fame was thereby obscured. Not that he cared. A man with half a million for his private income can be obscure in comfort

Page looked decidedly surprised when the manservant showed Alice and me into the well-appointed library. He was by the window, under the reading lamp, the light etching out his sharp features and neatly trimmed black torpedo-beard and moustache. One could easily have mistaken him for a Frenchman.

Getting to his feet he came over to us — a small, concise man with a perpetual slight smile that revealed the white of his teeth through his beard.

'Hello, Rod! Quite a little while since I've seen you.'

'Been busy,' I said, and promptly introduced Alice. This done, and the handshakes over, Page stood with his hands plunged in the pockets of his velvet smoking jacket whilst I gave him the story in detail. At the end of it he made no comment for a moment or two; then he looked at us with his small, keen blue eyes.

'Quite a remarkable story! Without any apparent explanation beyond the acquisition of a strange gem, you Miss Denham, start to lose weight and height, eh? Unique! Most unique! Let me have a look at it, Rod.'

I handed over the handkerchief containing the ring, and then added: 'Better take care how you deal with it!'

'I can assure you that I shan't take any chances. Come along with me, both of you.'

He led the way from his library to the small laboratory at the end of the hall. Floodlights came up automatically as the door opened. Removing the ring from the handkerchief with insulated forceps, Page put it under the electron microscope and peered intently. He spent nearly five minutes doing this, adjusting the instrument and murmuring under his breath. But the perpetual smile was still there when he glanced up.

'I assume,' he asked, 'that you are under the impression that the rays from this stone are simply prismatic light rays, like those of the diamond?'

'Well, aren't they?' I asked, surprised.

He shook his head, coming slowly forward. 'No. This gem is the most amazing thing upon which I have ever set eyes ... Most stones rely on their light-wave dissemination for their beauty — such as the diamond, ruby, sapphire, and so forth. On the other hand, stones of the opal class are absorptive of light. Here, however, is a gem of rare properties in that it radiates not only light waves but *cosmic* waves!'

Alice and I gazed, uncomprehending. Page continued:

'I hardly need to tell you, do I, that the air and space itself abound in different radiations such as heat, cosmic rays, radio waves, and so forth? So far we know of no mineral structure that will split up and radiate any of these radiations. Our limit is with stones which re-radiate light-waves with rare beauty. But here is a stone, apparently with *natural facets*, which re-radiates cosmic waves, and perhaps dozens of other radiations of which we know very little. It splits them up prismatically, hence the unholy lustre and the suggestion that here and there are colours we've never yet encountered. The dominant blue is, I think, caused by the breaking-up of ultra-violet; and the red is derived from infra-red.'

'But what has all this to do with Alice?' I demanded.

'I don't quite know — yet.' But I fancied from his expression that he did.

'Most certainly she had better not wear that ring again. I shall try to get a better light on its history from the jeweller from whom you bought it. The point is, that a stone like this able to re-radiate various waves may be utilizing some that are harmful to a human being. If the ring is no longer worn the trouble should cease . . . '

As he had been talking Page had led us back into the library. 'Now,' he continued seriously, 'you can rest assured that I'll find out all I can about it. The implications of this ring may be far-reaching. Now you have ceased to wear it, Miss Denham, I think you ought to be perfectly all right.'

'Well, that's something,' Alice admitted. 'But what about the stone in weight and two inches in height which have gone into nowhere? Will they return?'

'Candidly, I just don't know!'

Alice gave a rueful smile. 'Even at five feet two I always felt pretty small. Now I feel positively microscopic!'

'*Petite*, and as sweet as ever,' I smiled, my arm about her shoulders.

'If there *should* be any further developments, come and see me immediately,' Page advised. 'In fact, perhaps both of you had better drop in tomorrow evening and I'll be able to tell you how I've progressed.'

On that note we left matters. Alice said little as I drove her home, but I could tell that she was still very much alarmed. Nor was I much better myself. There had been something in Earl Page's manner, which to me — knowing him extremely well — had implied that he knew most of the truth but had not dared to tell it . . .

And the next day my alarm was sharpened considerably when immediately before I had set off for town, Alice rang me. Her voice was shaking with nervousness.

'Rod, I'm frightened! This business is still going on even though I haven't worn the ring! I've lost dimensions again in the night — I had some terrible dream, too. I seemed to be flying through space, or something — '

'I'll come right away,' I interrupted. 'Keep a grip on yourself, sweetheart. I'll soon be with you.'

I only stayed long enough to leave directions at the office, then I was on my way again to Alice's flat as fast as the car would go and this time, as she opened the door to me, I could behold the diminution clearly.

Alice's clothes were hanging baggily on her lessened figure. She was doll-like, fragile, and pitifully frightened. From her gaunt, weary face it was plain what sort of a night she had been through. The moment she saw me she caught hold of my arm and hung on to it as though afraid to let go.

'All right,' I murmured, embracing her gently. 'Take it easy, darling. We'll get this mess cleared up somehow. Let's go and see Page right away.'

When we arrived at Page's home he was in dressing gown and slippers, finishing his breakfast. His expression immediately became grim as his eyes traveled to Alice.

'Sit down, both of you . . . ' He called for extra coffee and then proceeded slowly. 'I called on the jeweler last evening but apparently he could not add anything to what you had already told me. I then browsed through the library and read up all I could find concerning gems — but without result. The 'Sunstone' is not even mentioned. So I had to fall back on an analysis of my own.'

The extra coffee was brought and Page resumed. 'I spent most of last night making tests. As I at first thought, the gem *does* transmit radiations of all kinds. If a low-powered radio beam is directed at it, it reflects it again as a mirror does light. Absolutely uncanny! However, from the gem there is radiating a wavelength of such exceptional smallness that I cannot place it even with instruments — unless I accept the most unbelievable proposition ever heard of!'

'And what's that?' I asked bluntly.

'That the wavelength is being generated

from somewhere inconceivably small and invisible to us. The wavelength also has a power that has a surprising effect on flesh-and-blood organisms. A white mouse which I put beside the ring for the night has *decreased in size*!'

Alice and I looked at each other anxiously. The coffee cups we were holding in our hands remained ignored.

'Strangely enough,' Page continued, 'the effect continues even when the ring is removed. That seems to show that once the effect — whatever it is — is absorbed into a living system it continues to exert its influence — '

'Then what happens to *me*?' Alice cried in horror. 'At least tell me that! I've got to know!'

Page came forward and looked down at her seriously. 'Believe me, Miss Denham, I wish I could give you the details, but for the moment I just don't know them. I'm fighting something I never even heard of before! I will be able to form a better prognosis when I have studied the final reactions of the mouse. In the meantime, if you can make arrangements to stay here, where I can keep you under observation, I may be able to do something for you. Think you can manage that?'

'Anything! Anything at all!'

'Good! I'll instruct my housekeeper to make the necessary arrangements. Be back here about noon with everything you require, then we'll go into the matter thoroughly.'

He accompanied us as far as the hall, scribbled something on a card, and pushed it into my pocket whilst Alice's back was turned. Once I had left Alice at her flat with the promise to return to her at noon after a call at the office, I read what had been written on the card. It was not reassuring.

Return immediately before Miss Denham. Very important that I should see you.

So, with dire expectations of something dreadful, I went back immediately to Page's home — and he wasted no time in coming to the point now Alice was not present to hear the details.

'Rod, your fiancée is unwittingly fighting something of baleful power! Unless my guess is entirely wrong, that jewel is being operated upon by powers in the microcosm.'

'Microcosm?' I repeated vaguely. 'I'm a stockbroker, Earl, not a scientist.'

'I'm sorry,' he apologized. 'I'm referring to the atomic world, which on an inconceivably small scale duplicates our known universe. It is quite possible that there might be highly intelligent beings in this microcosm, existing upon an electron. An electron cannot really be likened to a planet, of course, except for the purposes of analogy. However, since an electron is basically an electric charge, the only assumption we can draw is that the denizens of such an electron-world must *themselves* be electrical. Possibly even electric charges possessing intelligence.'

'Intelligent *electricity*? Damnit, man, that's stretching things a bit, isn't it?'

He smiled wistfully. 'Is it? We are intelligent electricity, too, remember! Maybe that startles you?'

It certainly did! Yet when I came to think of it I could see he was right. Everything material, including human and animal organisms, is based on electric forces. So after a while his idea did not seem so extraordinary after all.

'And you believe these electrical inhabitants of an electron world may be operating through the Sunstone?'

'I think so, yes. The action of the wavelength makes me think that, but the *purpose* of it I just do not understand! It is not remotely possible that Miss Denham was deliberately singled out. I think the whole thing was pure chance, and that she happened to be the recipient of these minute wavelengths.'

'And not only Alice,' I exclaimed, startled. 'All the other owners of the ring disappeared, too!'

'That,' Page said, 'is what is so disquieting.'

A thought suddenly struck me. 'What of the countless others who must have handled the gem? Even the jeweller himself for that matter! Nothing happened — least not to him.'

'As to that, they didn't have it continuously in contact with their flesh for over twelve hours. There was no effect on the mouse either until twelve hours had passed. I had the ring fastened tightly against its body, by the way. You will recall that only the *owners* of the ring have vanished — that is those who must have *worn* it. We do not hear anything untoward about those who transferred it from place to place.'

'Of all the damnable, horrific gems to be let loose in the world!' I breathed. 'It's more deadly than the most virulent poison! It's so — so utterly beautiful, yet so fiendishly diabolical!'

'Very true,' Page sighed, thinking.

'What you are telling me, Earl, is that somebody of incredible scientific ingenuity, living on an electronic charge — an electronic planet — deliberately sent that gem into our vastly greater universe and thereafter used it for the transmission of certain inexplicable wavelengths which cause shrinkage. Is that it?'

'That's it.'

'I don't see how that is possible.' I gave a frown. 'This gem must be countless millions of times larger than the world from which they sent it! How do you reconcile that?'

'There's a simple parallel,' he answered. 'Our modern scientists, by a play of vibrations upon certain mineral substances, can change the mineral gradually into a totally different atomic structure. For instance, they can change carbon into hard diamonds, and that's only one example . . . These electronic men of science, unseen, somewhere in the microcosm, have obviously transmitted from their world a series of vibrations to the extreme limit of their universe, knowing full well that beyond it must lie the greater macrocosm in which spins our world — '

'Why *our* world?' I interrupted. 'Are there not tens of millions of worlds to choose from?'

'Certainly, but ours — as far as we know at present — is the only one with human — I say *human* — life. Hence Earth was, I suggest, singled out. The concentrated force of those vibrations reacted on some part of our world, perhaps determined beforehand, to produce a combination of chemicals that formed into the Sunstone. That, I believe, is what happened . . . '

I must have looked very doubting, for Page added: 'The fact that they *can* do it is proved because they can still send vibrations through it even now, no matter where it is moved. That shows conclusively that the radiations are chained by some magnetic power or other to the jewel wherever it may be. Mighty science, Rod! Science pressed to its ultimate power for a reason we do not as yet understand. But we shall! I wanted to tell you all this in private. Once Miss Denham is with us again I may not have the opportunity and it would be nonsensical to alarm her unduly. By examination, tests, and research I may yet solve the mystery and save her.'

'There are no two ways about it!' I cried. 'The alternative to saving her is unthinkable!'

Page clapped me on the shoulder. 'We'll see what we can do — and needless to say, not a word to her!'

And so I departed to pick Alice up from her flat. I still do not know how I managed to keep a reasonably cheerful face on things, considering what I had heard. I was a victim to the knowledge that overwhelming forces had suddenly sprung into being, and the whole damned issue of them seemed to be concentrated entirely on the woman I held most dear . . .

★   ★   ★

Naturally, I made arrangements so that I too could stay with Page and be beside Alice in case of urgent need. There was at least a cold yet reassuring efficiency about Page, which was wonderfully heartening to both Alice and me. Indeed, her understandable fears abated considerably under Page's calm watchfulness.

From noon onwards until early evening he was the perfect host, never once mentioning the matter closest to our minds — but in that time I noticed how skillfully he wormed his way into Alice's confidence, how he watched her constantly whilst not appearing to be doing so, how his adding-machine brain made a note of her every movement and reaction.

We dined at seven, talked for another hour, and then at Page's suggestion went to the laboratory. Immediately he went into action. With his quick, capable hands he set about arranging his instruments, asking for and receiving the fullest co-operation from Alice. Neither of us understood much of what he did, though we certainly watched in fascinated interest . . . He used X-ray screens and took several plates; he tied elastic bandages around Alice's arm, in the fashion of a blood-pressure test — the difference being that in this case he attached electrodes to the bandage and then stood watching pensively as needles jumped in a panel of dials. He made notes by the score and went to work with other machines that bristled with tubes, wires, insulator banks, and multiple switches.

His final experiment did not concern Alice at all but the frightened and very much shrunken white mouse, and lastly the Sunstone itself. That deadly gem still shone with its unholy and transcendently beautiful lustre.

At last Page was finished. He stood

with his hands plunged in the pockets of his velvet jacket, beard touching his chest as he pondered.

'The facts,' he said finally, 'are not reassuring! There is nothing to be gained by evasion.'

'Nothing at all,' Alice agreed quietly, a tremor in her voice. 'What is it all about, Dr Page? Since I am the victim I am entitled to know. I don't want promises or put-offs. I simply want to know, where I stand.'

'It is only because I think I might be able to save you that I am going to tell you what is happening,' Page replied. 'In the first place, Miss Denham, the electric content of your body is three times that of normal. You did not know that, did you?'

'I certainly didn't. Would it explain a slight feeling of cramp all over me?'

'A mild pins-and-needles effect? Yes, that would explain it. Because you had that gem in close contact with your body for over twelve hours certain wavelengths have operated through it — wavelengths generated from somewhere in what we call the microcosm . . . ' Page went into

191

an explanation very similar to the one he had given me, except that it was 'watered down' especially not to frighten Alice too much; then he continued:

'This radiation has altered the normal electrical content of your body to such an extent that there is a distinct magnetism. I cannot work out the exact intricacies involved, but it seems that this magnetism is causing a closing-up of the electronic orbits that make up the molecular units of your body. As they close, you shrink, and *also* — by some means I don't understand — evidently lose weight and mass as a byproduct of the process. Is that clear?'

Alice nodded, even though she looked completely bewildered. 'Then what makes it progress? Why didn't it cease once the ring was taken out of the way?'

'Because the effect was by then stabilized. The electric content had been supplied to cause the alteration and it simply goes on functioning. Therefore, we must set to work to find a counteractive radiation that will arrest the trouble, or at least produce a negative result on the extra electricity absorbed into your body. Somehow we will find it, Miss Denham. Don't worry! This whole business has been devised by a brilliant science for an obscure reason, but I've one or two ideas of my own yet to try out . . . '

Page stood for a moment or two, considering, then he said: 'I believe you mentioned you had strange dreams last night?'

'I did, yes, and I cannot understand what they meant. It seemed to me as though I were falling endlessly through space. I could see the stars and great abysses of dark. Then there were huge, empty worlds . . . ' Alice gave a wistful smile. 'It made me feel just like a goddess looking down on the universe!'

'Mmmm. As a scientist, Miss Denham, it sounds to me more like a definite telepathic contact, between worlds. Telepathy takes no cognizance of distance and some kind of contact might be established between yourself and this unknown spot in the microcosm . . . From here on, Miss Denham, take careful note of your dreams. Write down every detail of them the moment you wake up, no matter how trivial those details may seem. Everything helps . . . For the moment I think that is all we can do. Tonight I shall work out a plan of attack to neutralize the trouble. Do all you can to sleep well, and if you don't I'll fix a sedative for you.'

It was more than evident to me that Page wanted to hurry both of us off to our rooms. I waited about my own room for nearly an hour after bidding Alice good night; then I returned downstairs to the laboratory. Sure enough Page was there, as I had expected, a long pipe smoldering between his bearded lips, his compact figure bent over the brightly lighted writing desk.

He merely glanced up and nodded to me, then went on working. Every now and again he got to his feet and set to work with electrical apparatus. There were satanic cracklings of energy, the air becoming tainted with the odor of ozone discharges. Once or twice he tried putting the diminutive mouse in a glass tube between anode and cathode and subjected it to a bombardment of unknown forces. The mouse appeared unharmed, but evidently the effect was not what Page desired for I saw he was becoming increasingly irritated.

'It's damnable!' he muttered at last, and threw down the pencil on his desk.

I looked at him morosely. 'I could think of an even stronger word than that, Earl!'

'I'm talking about this microcosmic world, wherever it is, and the fiendish inhabitants thereon! They must possess scientific knowledge far greater than ours. Why, they're even using a form of electrical energy that I just don't understand! And that, from me, is *some* admission!'

It certainly was! Earl Page was one of the foremost electrical wizards of his time even if he did keep his genius to himself.

'Like groping in the dark!' Page banged his fist on the desk.

I looked at him again. 'Look, Earl, do you mean by all this that Alice is — '

'I don't mean anything yet for certain.' His voice was sharp with frustration. 'I've tried to neutralize the mouse and you can see for yourself what's happened. The poor little devil still goes on shrinking! Look at it!'

I looked. Then I said mechanically, 'There must *be* a way, somehow! You'll find it, Earl. I'm sure you will!'

'You mean you *hope* I will! So far I have had nothing but failure to offer and upstairs there is that poor girl relying on my addled brains to save her from — ' Page checked himself. 'We don't know what from. That's probably the worst part of the whole business.'

'Suppose,' I said deliberately, forcing myself to speak words that were utterly deadening to me, 'no cure can be found and Alice just . . . fades away? How long will the process take?'

'No idea. If she reacts as the mouse has there is no predictable speed to the shrinkage. Sometimes it is slow, sometimes fast — but it's always *there!* It never stops.'

There was a long silence between us. Page lighted his pipe and drew at it savagely, his brows down, his face a pool of darkness under the diagonal rays of the desk-lamp. I turned the whole horrific business over in my mind and finally arrived at what seemed to me a logical inference.

'You say it is some form of electrical energy which is causing the orbits of the electrons forming Alice's body to shrink? Well, can't you find the opposite wave-length — or whatever it is — and make them expand?'

'That's what I have been trying to do, but it's like trying to work out a sum without knowing the basic principle of mathematics. I keep *telling* you, man, this electrical energy is not of the same type as we're familiar with.'

'I can't understand that at all, Earl. Surely electrical energy is the same throughout the universe? Positive and negative and — '

He interrupted me with a dry chuckle. 'We once thought the electron radiated energy, and that this would make it describe a continually decreasing orbit until it would spiral down into the nucleus and cause the whole atom to vanish in a flash of radiation. We *once* thought that, I say, until Niels Bohr came along with his quantum theory and showed that an electron whilst rotating in its orbit does not in fact radiate any energy whatever! It only radiates energy when jumping from one orbit to another, and the energy thus radiated is a quantum . . . So you see, if one supposed form of radiant energy can be supplanted so easily by another, why cannot electricity as such be in far more forms than the one *we* know? Come to think of it, electrical energy in a microcosmic universe probably *would* be very different from ours. Different laws. Different balance . . . The whole thing's plain hell, Rod!'

From here on he took so little notice of me, seemed indeed rather distracted by my presence, I took myself off to my room again. But as I passed along the dim corridor past Alice's room I paused and listened. I could hear her talking — or rather mumbling — at intervals, obviously as she slept. I pressed closer to the door and tried to catch the words.

' . . . shall be found and taken away . . . So vast and barren and alone . . . The machines! The robots! The cities! So far away . . . So far away . . . So small and yet so mighty!'

Then silence for a long while and deep breathing. At length I swung and raced quickly back to the laboratory to tell Page.

'Well, we obviously can't wake her,' he said briefly. 'But we might hear plenty with this . . . ' He picked up a wafer-flat microphone attached to a small portable tape recorder. Once we were upstairs again he pushed the microphone under Alice's bedroom door and then we both kept a silent vigil in the gloom, our faces faintly lighted by the green glow from the recorder's volume control. When presently the volume indicator began to jump on its green dial we both slipped on subsidiary headphones and listened to Alice's amplified voice as the recording was made.

' . . . the city covers the planet. The last man is dead but the robots live on . . . Even the robots must die unless they make a being of flesh-and-blood who will grow into an intelligent, reasoning creature and supply them with the life-force to make them anew . . . '

Long pause. The night wind sighed gently against the big window on the corridor. Down in the hall the big clock struck two.

'Looks as though we might be getting some idea of what really is the basis of all this,' Page muttered, dragging at his extinguished pipe. 'I don't like the sound of it, either! Robots needing a flesh-and-blood creature! It sounds — '

'She's talking again!' I interrupted.

' . . . robots follow out the commands of the flesh-and-blood master who is dead . . . They must have human life — flesh-and-blood . . . The microcosm is empty of life. But there is life on Earth. A mighty world is Earth, huge beyond imagining. One living being from that world and life can be manufactured from it, unit by unit. Unit by unit . . . '

A jumbled mumbling and then: 'Once I am small enough they will take me in an intra-atomic ship, bear me across the gulf to their own strange world. By then I shall be little more than an electrical charge, but the flesh-and-blood basis will still remain . . . '

The words drifted off. Page waited for what seemed an interminable time; then he silently withdrew the microphone, and switched off the instrument. With a silent movement of his head he indicated that I should follow him to the laboratory where we could talk in our normal voices.

'Looks to me as though we're really up against it!' he said bitterly. 'Those vague statements were obviously begotten of a telepathic contact with the microcosm, such as I theorized at first.'

'Evidently,' I admitted worriedly.

'Seems clear enough what is wrong,' Page continued after a moment. 'A race of robots — or at least they evidently seem that way to poor Alice's distracted mind — on a microcosmic world cannot continue indefinitely without a reasoning flesh-and-blood creature — or creatures. Following out the orders of the last flesh-and-blood master they have got to find more living matter from which to manufacture the life-force that animates them. There is apparently no life anywhere in their realm, so they have turned to this Earth of ours — hence the creation of the Sunstone; hence the disappearance of the previous owners thereof; hence the remorseless shrinkage of Alice Denham.'

'What happened to the previous owners of the Sunstone, do you suppose?' I asked. 'Did these microcosmic scientists get them? If so, why aren't they satisfied? Why keep on trying to get more flesh-and-blood?'

'I don't know for sure,' Page responded, 'but I have thought of one rather horrifying possibility. Miss Denham spoke of a race of robots that needed life-force to animate them: she also spoke of there being no life in the microcosm. It could be that this race has *denuded* the microcosm of all life, and are now having to turn to Earth to replenish their supply. As to why they are *continuing* their activities, it may be because of the different time-ratio. A few hours in our universe must be centuries to them; they must be using up the energy of living beings as fast as that damnable ring can supply them!'

I was too horrified to make any comment to this. Alice had mentioned 'units'. That could mean . . . vivisection! After a moment my gaze wandered from Page's troubled face to where the Sunstone was lying beyond him. It still lay on the bench not far from the greatly shrunken white mouse. A thought struck me, though I had no idea whether it was logical or not.

'According to your theory, Earl, once the gem has been in contact with the flesh for over twelve hours it produces an electrical effect which is progressive, whether the stone continues in contact or not?'

'That's right — and it's obvious my theory is correct.'

'Are you *sure*, though? Is it not perhaps possible that the stone radiates or transmits its queer energy over an enormous distance and thereby sort of keeps replenishing the mysterious energy which it has imparted to the 'subject'?'

'Most improbable, I'd say. Why, what have you in mind?'

'I was thinking we might isolate the

gem completely, surround it with a lead wall or something, to stop any radiation getting through. Would that work?'

'It might. Matter of fact I have a lead container that was used recently for radium needles. It might suit our purpose.'

'Try it!' I urged. 'Nothing is too fantastic at a time like this. We can soon see if it has any effect on the mouse.'

So we went to work — or rather Page did. Handling that terrible jewel was a task I preferred to leave to him alone, so I stood watching as with his insulated forceps he transferred the stone to the interior of the lead container and then clamped down the lid.

'By all normal laws this *should* block all radiation,' he said, thinking. 'The trouble is that I still don't know what kind of a radiation it is — even if it is radiation at all! I believe it's a form of electrical energy — '

'Makes no difference,' I interrupted. 'That container will still block it, won't it?'

'Definitely!'

So we started to watch the mouse as it moved with mournful slowness about its cage. There was none of the bright-eyed scampering usually attached to such a rodent. Just listless movements, and the obvious government of fear. Presently, since there was nothing we could do for a while, we went into the house proper and had some refreshment. It succeeded in partly chasing away our tiredness; then we returned into the laboratory and studied the mouse intently. Quietly, Page picked up the nearby ruler, lifted the mouse from its cage and laid it alongside the inches scale.

His face grim, he dropped the rodent back in the cage and closed the lid.

'Still shrinking,' he said.

Those words were to me an actual physical shock: I had been so sure my theory was the right one. Yet, just as quickly a new thought came, and I wondered why I had not grasped it before.

'Earl! How's this for another idea? The world from which this infernal energy, or whatever it is, is emanating, may actually be within the stone itself!'

He gave a slight start. 'Why, yes,' he murmured softly. 'I never thought of that. More than probable, in fact, which would explain how it is always kept in focus. Not only that world but its universe, and maybe a myriad other universes besides.'

'Destroy the stone utterly by electricity and we destroy that electronic world,' I said solemnly. 'Stockbroker I may be, but I *can* grasp that much!'

He hesitated no more. Quickly taking the gem from the container — once again with insulated forceps — he put it in the matrix of the atomic equipment. It seemed mighty force to use upon so small an object — the smashing of the nut with the sledgehammer indeed! — but the purpose merited it. Switches closed. For nearly ten minutes energy built up — then Page released it by throwing the switches. The Sunstone vanished in unholy fire and cascades of electrical energy, and to both of us it was a sombre thought that maybe thousands — millions — of universes in the microcosm had been destroyed in that instant.

'Now!' Page breathed, moving back to the rodent. 'Let us see . . . I still think the energy once absorbed is irreversible and continuous. But we can hope . . . '

In an hour we knew the answer. The mouse was three inches less in size . . .

The morning showed that Alice was visibly smaller. Breakfast was an almost silent affair, neither Page nor I saying what we had been doing in the night. He still seemed to think there was something he could try.

What I found particularly hard to endure was the dumb look of terror in Alice's eyes. I tried to reiterate assurances — but as the hours flew by and Page labored to master a science centuries ahead of him, my hopes began to sink into my boots. Evidently the energy *was* progressive, for it was still operating even though we had probably destroyed the original creators of it. This again was an awful thought. Alice had muttered something in her sleep about being picked up in an inter-atomic ship. That might now never be. Where in the devil's name *would* she go if we could not save her? If *we* could not. Egoist! The whole thing relied, as before, on Page.

Alice could see that we were fighting the impossible — and Page left no channel unexplored. He called in other scientists, and once they realized the astounding implications they threw all their combined genius into an effort to overcome the devilish power that was reducing the silent Alice before their fascinated eyes.

Hour by hour now, Alice was changing incredibly. She went to her room and I was the only one whom she would permit to see her. I gave her the news of the grim battle we were fighting, and *still* I tried to assure her that we would yet win the battle. Her only response was to smile faintly. She lay there in the bed, overcome now by a tremendous lethargy, which all the drugs sent up by Page failed to break. Yes, she lay there, like a waxen doll, and when I looked down on her I openly cursed that heinous stone we had seen in the jeweler's window.

I could not remember meals, or periods of rest, or anything. I was flying up and down stairs all the time. Until at length it was early evening and I realized that all the feverish activity of the day was over. The scientists had departed and Page sat in the laboratory, his dead pipe forgotten between his teeth.

Presently he looked up at me. 'It's no good, Rod! We've got to tell her — even if she doesn't know already. We're beaten! The latest reports from the other workers show that there is no known way of fighting this mysterious electrical force which, once infused into a living organism, causes the electronic orbits to shrink, and shrink and *shrink!*'

I stirred slowly as I stood before his desk. 'Somehow I had thought, even to the last, that you'd pull something out of the hat.'

'I'm not a magician, Rod.' He gave my arm a brief grip. 'Sometimes there drifts into the orbit of science a power, an unknown factor, which is completely beyond analysis. This is one of those times.' He got to his feet and put a hand to his forehead. 'God, but I'm weary . . . We'd better go and break the news as gently as we can.'

We went solemnly from the laboratory, through the hall, and up the stairs. When we had reached the corridor I caught hold of Page's arm.

'Earl — a moment. We can't tell Alice a terrible thing like this without giving her a way out. You've got dozens of potent, painless drugs down in that lab of yours. Can't you use one so that she . . . '

He hesitated. 'That would be euthanasia,' he said.

'I don't care!' I told him brutally. 'Every court in the land would uphold a mercy killing in a case like this! I insist on it, Earl. I'll take the responsibility!'

He looked at me steadily, then without another word he went back down the corridor. Quietly I entered Alice's room and took a few steps forward, leaving the door open.

I stopped. There was a deadly quietness in the evening light. Outside the window the newly budding beech tree swayed in the evening breeze . . . I absorbed the merciless, overwhelming fact that the bed was empty! There were the tangled clothes, the sewn-in nightdress, which Alice had contrived to fit her diminishing proportions . . . And that was all.

At the sound of swift footsteps I turned and looked fixedly towards the doorway as Page came in, a phial in his hand. He looked at me, at the bed, and back to me.

'We shan't need that now,' I said in a low voice.

Outside the window the beech tree swayed and was straight again . . .

THE END

CLIMATE INCORPORATED
THE FIVE MATCHBOXES
EXCEPT FOR ONE THING
BLACK MARIA, M.A.
ONE STEP TOO FAR
THE THIRTY-FIRST OF JUNE
THE FROZEN LIMIT
ONE REMAINED SEATED
THE MURDERED SCHOOLGIRL
SECRET OF THE RING
OTHER EYES WATCHING
I SPY . . .
FOOL'S PARADISE
DON'T TOUCH ME
THE FOURTH DOOR
THE SPIKED BOY
THE SLITHERERS
MAN OF TWO WORLDS
THE ATLANTIC TUNNEL
THE EMPTY COFFINS
LIQUID DEATH
PATTERN OF MURDER
NEBULA
THE LIE-DESTROYER
PRISONER OF TIME

MIRACLE MAN
THE MULTI-MAN
THE RED INSECTS
THE GOLD OF AKADA
RETURN TO AKADA
GLIMPSE
ENDLESS DAY
THE G–BOMB
A THING OF THE PAST
THE BLACK TERROR
THE SILENT WORLD
DEATH ASKS THE QUESTION

We do hope that you have enjoyed reading this large print book.

Did you know that all of our titles are available for purchase?

We publish a wide range of high quality large print books including:
Romances, Mysteries, Classics
General Fiction
Non Fiction and Westerns

Special interest titles available in large print are:
The Little Oxford Dictionary
Music Book, Song Book
Hymn Book, Service Book

Also available from us courtesy of Oxford University Press:
Young Readers' Dictionary
(large print edition)
Young Readers' Thesaurus
(large print edition)

For further information or a free brochure, please contact us at:
Ulverscroft Large Print Books Ltd.,
The Green, Bradgate Road, Anstey,
Leicester, LE7 7FU, England.
Tel: (00 44) **0116 236 4325**
Fax: (00 44) **0116 234 0205**

Other titles in the
Linford Mystery Library:

MR. BUDD STEPS IN

Gerald Verner

Somewhere in England is a steel box — its contents more valuable than diamonds — that Superintendent Robert Budd must find. Budd's investigation takes him to Higher Wicklow, where a tramp had sheltered in its reputedly haunted mill. Some days later, his body was discovered, his throat cut. Although the coroner's verdict was suicide, the villagers believe there's a more sinister explanation. Can the Superintendent discover the truth? Budd's heavy caseload also includes murder, ghostly goings on, a vanishing and blackmail.

THE DARK GATEWAY

John Burke

In a lonely corner of Wales, an ancient castle quivers with evil as menacing powers return from beyond ... The family living on the hillside farm with their daughter, Nora, has a stranger coming to live with them. But he's not what he seems — he will not fulfil Nora's hopes of romance ... As the powers of darkness approach, the human race is in danger and the earth itself is at stake. In this frightened community, who will oppose the invaders?

UNDER THE KNIFE

Steve Hayes and David Whitehead

A vicious serial killer haunts the bayous of Louisiana. The only person who can catch him is FBI Agent Kate Palmer. But Kate's specialised work has taken its toll on her and she's facing burnout. Worse still, she's about to rekindle a relationship with the only man she ever loved when the Bayou Butcher strikes again — terrifyingly close to home. For Kate, that makes it personal — it might also be just the thing it takes to break her completely.